2
1 4

A Most Rebellious Debutante

A Most Rebellious Debutante

Karen Abbott

ROBERT HALE · LONDON

© Karen Abbott 2010
First published in Great Britain 2010

ISBN 978-0-7090-9031-1

Robert Hale Limited
Clerkenwell House
Clerkenwell Green
London EC1R 0HT

www.halebooks.com

2 4 6 8 10 9 7 5 3 1

Typeset in 11.2/16.5pt New Century Schoolbook
Printed in Great Britain by the MPG Books Group, Bodmin and King's Lynn

Dedicated in memory of my dear dad,
Bernard Mitchell, 13.10.1913–24.12.2008.
'If there's a window in heaven, I know you are
looking down, enjoying this moment.'

Also to the RNA for their unwavering encouragement.

One

SEATED ON A padded window seat overlooking the beautifully landscaped grounds of her home, seventeen-year-old Lucy Templeton presented a picture of studied elegance. Her chestnut hair was caught high in loose ringlets at the back of her head, held in place by a perfectly tied blue satin bow, the ends of which trailed down her cascading tresses. A few tendrils fell alluringly in front of her ears as she posed with her legs curled beneath the folds of her sprigged muslin gown, her head inclined towards the open copy of Walter Scott's recently published *Lady Of The Lake* that she held in one hand.

A casual observer might have presumed her to be engrossed in her book ... but, if she were observed for any length of time, it would be noticed that her other hand rarely moved to turn the page and, every so often, she sighed with impatience and leaned nearer to the window-pane. Where *was* he? He ought to have been here by now!

'He'll be here soon, miss,' her maid, seated on a chair a few feet away, assured her, glancing up from her sewing.

'Yes, I know, Susie ... but I do so hate to wait. Don't you?'

'Oh, aye, miss,' Susie responded wryly, knowing that her

young mistress had no notion of the hours her maid spent awaiting her mistress's commands.

'Oh!'

Lucy's heartbeat suddenly quickened as a sporting curricle appeared in the distance where the curve of the drive first allowed visitors a glimpse of the mellow stone house. The spinning wheels of the delicately hung curricle churned the smaller particles of crushed stone into clouds of dust as the driver wildly tooled his vehicle around the curve. He was here! Even at that distance she knew it was he!

Abandoning all pretence of reading, Lucy pressed her face to the cool glass of the window and avidly drank in every nuance of movement of the young driver, gasping with admiration as he flicked his long whip over the back of his matching greys, imagining rather than hearing the sharp crack, knowing that he considered himself to be a 'capital whip', and relished her adoring admiration of this feat.

She giggled at the sight of his passenger, nervously gripping the side of his seat with his left hand and clutching his violin to his chest with the other. She'd bet his face was as white as his shirt.

Her gaze followed the progress of the recklessly driven curricle as it approached the imposing frontage of Alverston Hall, craning her neck to watch the curricle come to a halt in front of the curved stone steps that led up to the magnificent pillared portico. The driver leaped from his seat and tossed the reins into the hands of the waiting footman before bounding up the steps. Only then did Lucy slip off the window seat.

'He's here!' she breathed unnecessarily, crossing the room

to her bedroom door. Although she longed to run along the landing and down the magnificent stairway, she didn't immediately do so. Instead, she paused on the landing and smoothed out the creases of her gown ... then lightly patted her cheeks with her cool hands in an effort to dispel some of the heightened colour. Hearing the murmur of male voices drifting up from the entrance hall below, she leaned over the balustrade and peered down upon the white bewigged head of Hartley, the first footman, as he took the beaver hat that the dark-haired young man was holding out to him.

'Mario!' Lucy breathed silently.

As if he had heard her, Mario glanced upward, but Lucy had already withdrawn her head, smiling with delight as she did so. She didn't need to see him. She knew every contour of his bronzed face, his finely boned cheeks, his smooth forehead, his chin ... and his twinkling dark eyes that she just *knew* were, at this moment, glancing upwards, hoping to see her admiring gaze.

For a second, a tiny frown puckered her face. She knew she oughtn't to let her adoration be so obvious. Mama said that young ladies of good breeding held their feelings in check, but she couldn't help it. She loved him so!

'Miss Lucy?'

Hartley had silently ascended the stairway.

'Your dancing master has arrived, Miss Lucy. Lady Templeton bids you and your maid join her in the music room.'

'Thank you, Hartley.'

She turned to face her maid. 'How do I look, Susie? Is my hair in place? Is my dress all right?'

'You look fine, miss ... not that Signor Vitali would notice

9

if you weren't.' She sighed, looking as dreamy-eyed as her mistress. 'Ooh, he's lovely, ain't he, miss?'

'He is indeed, but don't let Mama see that you think so, or she will bring back that dowdy old Mr Harris out of his retirement … and just think how dull *that* would be!'

Giggling at the thought, the two young women lightly descended the staircase, but paused outside the open door of the music room to compose their features … and it was with downcast eyes that they entered the room.

'Ah, Lucy! Signor Vitali is here to commence your dancing lesson,' Lady Templeton greeted her younger daughter. 'Look sharp now, for you know we are to make calls later this afternoon!'

'Yes, Mama,' Lucy murmured demurely, her eyes still cast down, knowing full well that her dark eyelashes fanned alluringly across her cheeks as she did so.

'You have left us little time to make our preparations for our calls, *signor!*' her mama continued coolly, her gaze as frosty as her tone. 'I fear that I am unable to stay beyond these first few minutes … but, no matter. Susie will act as chaperon on my behalf.'

The slender figure of the dancing master made an elaborate bow, his left hand held behind his back, his right hand flourishing an intricate pattern in the space between himself and the upright figure of Lady Templeton.

'My sincere apologies, *signora*. My preceding pupil … she needs much extra tuition. She ees not as responsive as your delightful daughter. As for you, *signora*, you need no time at all to make preparations of beauty! You are a picture of delight to ze eyes of any man. And we Italianos … we love ze beauty of ze mature English rose!'

Lucy hid a smile at his words. Flatterer! He could charm the birds out of the sky! It was a wonder her mama fell for it! But a glance at her mama's face showed that Mario's charm had worked. Her mama's earlier chilly expression had given way to a glow of pleasure. Little did her mama know that his true admiration was for her daughter.

Mario turned towards Lucy, a warm gleam in his sparkling eyes. He made his bow and Lucy sank into a curtsy before him as if he were a royal duke at the Prince Regent's great Fête at Carlton House on 19 June, safe in the knowledge that it was part of her lesson.

Mario took hold of her hand and drew her to her feet, nodding to his violinist to strike up the music.

'We begin wiz a simple minuet, I think,' he murmured, holding her hand at the required height, squeezing her fingers gently, to remind her of his hidden love.

Her heart beating erratically, Lucy flickered a glance at him through her long, dark eyelashes, but instantly cast them down again. Not while Mama was still in the room!

Her body performed the delicate pattern of intricate steps while her heart raced with pleasure and delight. How fortunate she was to be able to hold the hand of her beloved under the eagle eye of her mama without incurring sharp censure. The very audacity of it heightened her excitement and she hardly knew how she kept her face suitably demure.

As they moved out of her mama's hearing, Mario's whispered endearments brought a faint blush to her cheeks. The words were in Mario's own language but she didn't need to know their exact translation in order to understand their meaning! They were words of love – a universal language!

By the time they were counting out the steps of a quadrille,

Lady Templeton had departed to her salon, leaving only Susie in attendance. Lucy concentrated on differentiating between the *chassés, jettés, glissades* and the *coupes de balance*, unaware that Mario had manoeuvred her into a far corner of the room where the caressing touch of his hand went unnoticed by her maid.

'Ah, you have such elegance and grace!' he murmured softly in her ear. 'Zere is a new dance zat I would like to teach you, *cara mia*. Eet ees called ze waltz. You have heard of eet?'

Lucy's eyes widened. 'Why, yes, but it is very daring, isn't it?' She grinned wickedly. 'Mama says it is far too strenuous for young ladies and will lead to fainting fits! But I am sure she is wrong. Can you teach it to me?'

'Oh, I would find eet a great pleasure, but it involves holding you in my arms. I fear your mama might be displeased.'

He looked so woebegone that Lucy laughed. 'She isn't here! And I'm sure Susie won't tell tales of me!'

'No, I have ze better idea! Leave eet to me.' He strode over to his musician and murmured some words that Lucy couldn't hear. He came back smiling.

'Come! We begin over here.'

He led her to the centre of the room and nodded to the violinist to begin. Smiling into her eyes, he lifted her right hand with his left and placed his right hand around her waist, drawing her closer to him.

Lucy gasped with pleasure. She was sure she could feel Mario's heart beating through the layers of clothing that separated them. Could he feel hers? They were beating the same rhythm, she was sure.

'Put your left hand on my shoulder,' Mario instructed her, adding softly in her ear, 'Press closer to me then you can sense which way to move. *Si*, just so! Now we begin. One two three. One two three. See! *Bellissimo*! Eet ees so easy!'

Lucy began to follow his steps, hesitantly at first, but, as she relaxed into the regular rhythm, she could feel the pressure of his thighs against hers directing her steps. It was heavenly. Her body felt as though it were liberated, moving under a power outside of herself as she felt herself being revolved round and round. Almost lost in the heady experience, she raised her eyes and was startled to find Mario's eyes were locked with hers. She felt as though she were drowning in the depth of his gaze. Surely, she was about to collapse in his arms? The ecstasy of it! Oh, no wonder mamas didn't want their daughters to learn this dance!

Suddenly, the violinist began to lose the rhythm and his playing came to an abrupt end as he bent over as a paroxysm of coughing seized him.

Awakened out of their trance-like feeling, Lucy felt a bewildered disappointment flow over her as their steps slowed and then stopped.

Mario waved an impatient hand towards Susie. 'You, girl, go to ze kitchen and get him a glass of water,' he commanded. 'Better still, take him with you.'

'But ... Miss Lucy?' Susie implored. 'I must stay here.'

The violinist began another fit of coughing, red in the face by now. Lucy felt quite concerned for him. 'Oh, do take him, Susie. The man is nearly choking. Look, I'll come—'

'No. Your maid can manage. He will be all right,' Mario restrained her. 'Go, girl, before he collapses.'

Very reluctantly, Susie opened the door and gestured to

the man to follow her. She cast a glance over her shoulder as she left the room but could see no alternative but to do as the dancing master had bidden her.

'What a shame, and we were doing so well!' Lucy exclaimed in disappointment, stepping away a little from her partner. 'Oh, what a wonderful dance! But are you sure it will be allowed in the salons? It seems very *risqué!*'

Mario laughed, his white teeth gleaming. 'You are one of ze first to dance it ... but it is gaining favour in private gatherings and will soon be danced in ze best of assembly rooms. It is under consideration wiz ze matriarchs of Almack's and I expect it to be accepted zere before too long. So, I am teaching my pupils so zat zey will be amongst ze first to perform ze dance in public! But no one has picked it up as quickly as you, *bella mia.*'

'Really?' Lucy's eyes sparkled. 'Oh, it was wonderful!'

She began to move by herself, her arms outstretched in the required position, twirling herself around and around, her eyes closed as if she were dreaming. She felt a hand about her waist and her right hand taken in hold again. Her eyes flew open to see Mario's smiling face just above hers.

'Who needs music?' he said lightly. 'It ees here in our hearts!'

He drew her close again and began once more to twirl her round and round. Laughing in delight, Lucy twirled and whirled in ever faster movements until she felt so dizzy she was sure she was about to fall.

'Oh, stop, stop!' she laughed, collapsing against him, laughing up into his smiling face.

'Ah, *cara mia!*' Mario breathed, raising his hand to her face, gently stroking her cheek with the tips of his fingers.

Lucy felt a shiver of delight run through her body. Oh, this was heaven! She loved him so much. She parted her lips to breathe his name and Mario lowered his face towards her. Lucy closed her eyes in anticipation of the touch of his lips upon hers—

'Lucy! Signor Vitali!' came enraged tones from the doorway. 'What is the meaning of this outrage? Release my daughter at once, *signor*!'

'Mama!' Lucy gasped, brought down to earth with a start, suddenly aware of the compromising position in which she was being held. She made an effort to step aside but was temporarily unable to do so and she realized that Mario was shocked into immobility by her mother's sudden appearance in the room.

'Mama, it is not as you think!' she insisted tremulously. 'It is a new dance and Mario says it will soon be danced at Almack's in Town.' she hastened to explain. 'It is from … from …'

'From Austria,' Mario obligingly supplied. 'It ees quite ze rage out zere, milady. Why, even royalty have been known to enjoy ze dance!'

Lady Templeton's eyebrows rose as her daughter made use of her dancing master's Christian name. 'I don't care if our own Prince Regent enjoys it!' she exclaimed, her wrath still apparent. 'Release my daughter from that unseemly hold at once, sir!'

Lucy slipped from within the circle of his arms and stepped towards her mama. 'But, Mama. We meant no harm!'

'Retire to your room, Lucy,' Lady Templeton commanded icily. 'And, you, *signor*, leave at once! I have grave misgivings about your suitability as my daughter's dancing master – indeed, as *any* young lady's dancing master … and I have no doubt that when Lord Templeton hears of this, there will be severe repercussions, as you will, no doubt, discover when I spread the word!'

'But, Mama! You can't! We are in love! Tell her, Mario! Tell her that we love each other!'

She flew back to him and seized hold of his hand before facing her mama again. 'We … we intend to be married!' she declared passionately.

Lady Templeton's eyebrows rose again. 'Indeed? And you, *signor*? You know that permission for that will never be granted!'

Mario bowed before her, a little less flamboyantly than earlier. However, a tiny smile hovered about his lips.

'I think I need to request an audience with Lord Templeton, milady,' he responded quietly.

Lucy's gasp of delight was stilled by her mother's icy reply.

'That request will not be granted, *signor*!'

'Oh, I think it will, milady. Don't forget that I, too, have the ear of many in society!'

Lucy was puzzled. What did he mean? She looked at him uncertainly.

He didn't meet her eyes. Instead, they were fixed on her mama's face, his lips slightly twisted by an inscrutable glimmer of a smile.

'Indeed?' Lady Templeton narrowed her eyes. She continued slowly, 'I think I have your measure, *signor*.'

'I am sure you do, milady.'

They eyed each other silently for a moment. Lady Templeton was the first to break the hold.

'Go to your room, Lucy. We will leave this in the hands of your father.'

Lucy looked uncertainly from her mother's face to Mario's. Mario's eyes remained fixed on her mother.

'Go now!' her mother repeated.

Mario made no move to restrain her and, stifling a lump that threatened to invade her throat, Lucy ran from the room. Her heart was in turmoil. Would Mario manage to convince her father? Would her father listen when she added her pleas?

But, even as she ran up the stairs, she was filled with unease. Why had Mario not echoed her declaration of love? Why would he not meet her gaze? He could at least have given his assurance that he would do his best to persuade her father to be sympathetic towards them, even if Papa insisted that they wait a year or so ... maybe until she had had her Season?

Filled with a premonition of dread, she flung herself on to her bed and allowed her tears to soak into her pillow. Susie did her best to comfort her.

'Eeh, Miss Lucy,' she murmured, over and over, as she stroked her hair and patted her shoulder.

Lucy lost all sense of time. Dusk was falling when she sat up and allowed her maid to comb through her tangled hair. She bore it for a short time but, impatient to know what was happening, Lucy soon pushed her hand away.

'Go and see if you can discover anything downstairs,' she commanded her maid. 'But try not to let yourself be seen.'

Susie returned within ten minutes.

'Lord Templeton has returned home,' she whispered

urgently, her voice filled with suppressed excitement. 'They are in his study!'

She hesitated, anxiously eyeing her mistress's face. 'I couldn't hear what they were saying, but Lady Templeton sounds very upset and Lord Templeton was shouting.'

'And Mario? What about him?'

'I couldn't hear his words – he didn't raise his voice – but each time he spoke, Lord Templeton shouted back.'

Lucy was hopeful. If Mario could keep himself calm, he might impress her papa with his propriety!

'Go back and listen again.'

It wasn't long before Susie scampered back into the room.

'He's going!' she whispered urgently. 'Quick! Go to the window!'

Lucy was in time to see Mario climb into his curricle and drive past the front of the hall. He flourished his whip and the position of his body did not imply that he was leaving in disgrace. He knew which window was hers and Lucy hoped he might lift his head to give her a sign of encouragement, but he didn't. She watched until he was out of sight, wondering when she would see him next. She was still seated in the window embrasure staring towards the end of the avenue when the door opened and her mama came into the room.

'He has gone!' she announced flatly. 'He will not trouble us again.'

'G … Gone?' Lucy echoed. 'For how long?'

'For ever, if he keeps his word. Not that men like him know anything about gentlemanly behaviour.'

'No! He will come back! He loves me! He will wait until I am older.' Lucy's hands were clenched at her sides as she tearfully faced her mama. 'He will, Mama! He will!'

Lady Templeton shook her head. Her face was no longer stern. Indeed, she seemed more saddened than angry. 'His love is for money, my dear,' she said softly. 'He threatened to create a scandal if we didn't pay him enough money to buy his silence. He has accepted a thousand pounds to ensure that he never seeks your presence again ... and our agreement that we will not speak of this incident to anyone. Oh, my dear!'

She held out her arms to her daughter but Lucy didn't move into her embrace. She felt her face drain of its blood and a cold hand seemed to clutch at her heart. She felt betrayed, but she wasn't sure whom she hated more – her parents for ensuring Mario's departure from her life, or Mario for accepting their bribe.

Two

LUCY SIGHED AS she stared disconsolately out of the window of the family town coach as it sped along the road taking her away from Alverston Hall. She didn't see the passing scenery: her heart was broken in two. She was destined to live and die as a loveless spinster, tolerated only because of her usefulness to entertain her nieces and nephews.

The heavy sigh caused her maid to look enquiringly at her young mistress, but Lucy made no move to reassure her that everything was all right. It *wasn't* all right! It would never be all right again. Her life may as well be over.

Indignation once more flooded through her as she recalled the embarrassing interview with her father, Edmund Lord Templeton. He had been outraged by her dance master's behaviour and had declared Signor Vitali to be a charlatan of the first order; a pretender, out to bamboozle his way into the unsuspecting households of Polite Society.

'And you were gulled by his flummery, Lucy,' he added censoriously. 'You must learn to distinguish between *le bon ton* and those whose aim is to worm their way into Society by the back door. I might hold only the title of baron but you know you will have a considerable fortune bestowed upon you on your marriage.'

'But money doesn't come into it, Papa! Mario and I love each other!' Lucy had declared passionately, her hands clasped at her breast, quite certain that her mama's outrage had caused her to misunderstand what had been said in her papa's study.

'Pah! *You* may imagine yourself to be in love, but Signor Vitali has his feet firmly planted on the ground. He made it very clear what *his* objective was, and bargained his way into a cool thousand pounds for his withdrawal!'

The repetition of the words hit Lucy as sharply as if her father had slapped her. 'I don't believe it!' she cried in anguish. 'He said he loved me!'

'Men like him are unprincipled!' Lord Templeton said contemptuously. 'They will smooth-tongue their way into the hearts of innocent young ladies like yourself who foolishly put themselves into jeopardy by flouting the safeguards that their parents and Society have put into place! You should not have sent your maid out of the room with his accompanist!'

'But the man was choking, Papa. What else was I to do?'

'You should have rung for Hartley. It was *his* vigilance that brought your mama so opportunely on to the scene. And what a scene! You were entwined in the man's arms – a moment later and he would have been kissing you! Have you no shame, Lucy?'

Lucy cast her eyes down. At the moment when Mario had swept her into his arms, she had been surprised but also delighted. He had whispered words of love in her ear on previous occasions and she had dreamed of him kissing her, but her mama's sudden appearance had prevented even that.

But, in reality, she knew it shouldn't have happened. She had thought herself in love – and that Mario was in love with her.

Her father's voice softened. 'You might find social conventions to be tiresome, Lucy, but they are there for your protection! That is why young ladies of your class in Society are carefully chaperoned and introduced only to *suitable* young men!'

But Lucy was still hurting and she didn't want to know who was deemed suitable or unsuitable. What did her papa know about falling in love? It was so unfair. 'So, I will have no say about whom I will be allowed to meet and marry,' she had said with deliberate disdain in her voice.

'Your wishes will, of course, be taken into consideration, but you must be guided by your mama and me. We have your best interest at heart. Next year, you are to have your Season in London and your mama will see that you are introduced to only the best of Society.'

Huh! The *best* and the *boring*! *No one* would match up to Mario!

'But what if I do not fall in love with any of them?' she persisted. 'If I cannot marry for love then I will *never* marry!'

Lord Templeton hid a faint smile at her passionate declaration.

'Falling in love is not essential for a happy marriage, Lucy. Liking and respect are often sufficient. In the meantime, your mama and I feel it is expedient for you to visit your sister for a month or so. The fresh country air will be beneficial to you at this time of year and Marissa will, no doubt, be happy for you to provide distractions for young Bertie and Arabella whilst she is in confinement.'

Lucy was dumbfounded. 'You are sending me away?'

'Only for a few weeks. It is for your own good.'

'You are hoping I will forget Mario, but I won't!'

'I assure you, he has already forgotten *you* and, no doubt, has his eye on another gullible miss! My only regret is that we cannot warn our contemporaries about his perfidious dealings. Unfortunately, *our* silence assures us of *his*.'

And in the two weeks since the unfortunate incident, Lucy reflected sadly, Mario Vitali had made no effort at all to contact her; not even a secretly passed note via her friend, Eliza Carlton, whom she knew was also a pupil of his.

And now, here she was, lumbering through the late summer countryside to her sister's home in Norfolk, feeling simply wretched. She had been abandoned by her would-be lover and cast out by her family, and would, no doubt, be an encumbrance to her elder sister, tolerated only for her usefulness during the final weeks of Marissa's confinement and would forever be the maiden aunt whom everyone despised. A second sigh escaped her lips, dragging Susie's gaze upon her once more.

'Don't be downcast, miss. You'll fall in love with someone else, someone more suitable.'

'No, Susie. My heart is broken. I am determined *never* to fall in love again.'

Lucy spent a few satisfying moments pondering the tragedy of her broken heart, but found it impossible to hold on to the negative declaration for any longer. With a surge of martyred optimism, she declared grandly, 'Instead, I will devote my life to helping unfortunate women who find themselves at the mercy of unscrupulous men.'

That momentous decision didn't entirely take away the heartache she was feeling, but at least it gave her a positive attitude to enable her to withstand any reproaches her sister and brother-in-law might toss her way.

As events turned out, she didn't even see her brother-in-law, The Honourable Rupert Cunningham, that day. It was late afternoon when the coach turned in at the wrought-iron gates of Glenbury Lodge and Lucy was glad the uncomfortable journey had finally come to an end. Every bone in her body felt as if it had been beaten and her head felt like a leaden ball that was becoming far too heavy for her neck to support.

An under-footman, who had obviously been keeping a lookout for them, ran down the stone steps and was ready to open the carriage door as soon as Thomas brought the carriage to a halt. He let down the step as Lucy rose from her seat.

'I'll see you later, Susie,' she said to her maid. 'Make sure all my baggage is carried upstairs carefully and order some hot water to be taken to my room for a bath. A nice long soak before dinner will be just the thing!'

She descended from the carriage and looked to where Farrell, her brother-in-law's butler, was standing at the top of the steps ready to receive her. Lifting the hem of her carriage gown she ascended towards him, her head held high.

'Good afternoon, Farrell,' she greeted him cordially as he bowed his bewigged head.

'Good afternoon, Miss Templeton. Welcome back to Glenbury Lodge.'

Lucy began to draw off her gloves, glancing around the familiar reception hall. She was surprised to see her sister emerge from the drawing room to greet her, instead of waiting for her to be announced. She smiled and moved towards her, but Marissa held out a hand, warding her off.

'Lucy, dear, don't come any nearer, I beg of you. It became apparent only yesterday that my darling Bertie has contracted chickenpox and I fear Arabella is sickening for it, too, as she is so hot and irritable. I cannot remember you having had it and I dare not run the risk of returning you to Mama with your face marked with pox scars just a few months before your Season.'

Lucy stilled the hand that was about to draw off her second glove. 'Then, what am I to do, Marissa? Am I to return home? Only, it is rather late and my whole body aches from the uncomfortable journey as it is.'

'Dear me, no!' Marissa laughed. 'Since it was too late to put off your visit, I have arranged for you to spend a week or so with a near neighbour, the Countess of Montcliffe. Did you meet her or the dowager countess on your previous visits? Probably not, as you weren't then out of the school-room. Lady Montcliffe doesn't entertain a great deal at the moment, but she is willing to have you stay, owing to our difficult circumstances. And don't worry, my dear, neither of her sons is in residence at present.'

Lucy recalled the tales she had heard of the wild escapades of the two sons of the late Earl of Montcliffe. Her most vivid memories of the two brothers concerned their wild dashes through the countryside and the nearby village on their fine thoroughbreds, and the whispered tales she overheard about their equally wild behaviour in the local taverns and beyond. She fleetingly thought it might be quite exciting if one or other of them *were* in residence, but then she remembered her broken heart and decided that she would prefer to live in seclusion until it mended, for how could she mourn her lost love if she were being daily entertained by a hot-blooded buck?

'I am sorry to send you on your way so swiftly, Lucy,' she realized Marissa was saying to her, 'but Lady Montcliffe and the dowager countess keep country hours and I don't want your late arrival to cause their ladyships any discomfort. I will send for you as soon as Dr Walmsley says our household is free of infection. Give Lady Montcliffe and the dowager countess my felicitations, Lucy, and I will see you as soon as I am able. Goodbye, my dear.'

And so, with no more ado, Lucy was escorted back down the steps by Farrell and handed up into her carriage once more. She flopped down upon the seat she had vacated less than ten minutes previously feeling more than a little sorry for herself. Did *nobody* really want her?

Montcliffe Hall was a large mellow stone building that nestled against a backdrop of trees and was surrounded by well-kept gardens. A large rectangular pool was the centrepiece. Its edges were flagged, with small statuettes and stone urns placed at regular intervals along the two longer sides, creating an avenue that drew the eye to the front of the house. In the centre of the pool, a magnificent fountain played. It all looked so grand that Lucy began to feel a little nervous, but she need not have worried. Lady Montcliffe received her very graciously.

She was a slender, elegant lady of middle years, dressed in a gown of royal-blue sarsnet, the colour of which perfectly matched her eyes. She was still a beautiful woman and her dark hair was styled in a modish fashion.

'Welcome, my dear,' she said, in a melodious voice. 'I hope you will be happy for the duration of your visit. It will be like a breath of fresh air to have someone young around the place … and you must treat Montcliffe Hall as your home whilst you are with us. Now, if you will go upstairs with Mrs Grant, I think you will find that all is ready for your maid to help you change out of your travelling clothes. We are dining informally at present as only myself and the dowager countess are in residence.'

Lucy followed the housekeeper along the wide, brightly lit reception hall and up a curved staircase adorned with a variety of oil paintings and then along a number of passages until the housekeeper paused and opened a door.

'Here is your room, Miss Templeton. When you have bathed and changed, instruct your maid to ring the bell and someone will come to take you to the small dining room.'

Lucy was thankful of the chance to refresh herself in the hot bathtub. Her boxes had already been delivered to her room and Susie had hung most of her gowns when she emerged from the tub to be engulfed in a wondrously soft bath towel. Laid upon the bed was a pair of drawers, a chemise, a corset and a full-length petticoat.

'I think we're going to like it here, Miss Lucy,' Susie commented, as she dressed her mistress in the layers of underwear. 'And maybe this round-gown, since there's no company?' she suggested, holding up a gown of a dark-cream lawn that was one of Lucy's favourites.

Thus attired, Lucy was eventually escorted to the dining room, where Lady Montcliffe smiled her welcome. The table was set for two, each chair with a liveried footman in attendance, and the countess directed Lucy to her seat, explaining that the dowager countess preferred to eat upstairs in her suite of rooms. 'But you and I shall eat together, Miss Templeton … or may I call you Lucy?'

'Oh, please do, Lady Montcliffe. That will make me feel much more at home.'

The dinner was a pleasant meal, consisting of a bowl of cream of celery soup with a freshly baked bread roll, followed by a fillet of steamed turbot in a butter sauce, which was then removed with a selection of hot meats and vegetables with accompanying sauces.

Lucy glanced around as the various covers were removed and replaced. Her eyes lighted upon two portraits that adorned the wall above the fireplace. Each was of a handsome dark-haired young man in military uniform.

Lady Montcliffe followed her glance. 'They are my sons,' she said, with pride in her voice. 'The one on the left is Theo, the eldest … and the one on the right is Conrad, just one year younger. Oh, how I miss them.'

'Are they still fighting in the Peninsular War?' Lucy asked, wondering if the infamous Earl of Montcliffe and his younger brother were likely to remain absent for the whole duration of her stay.

'Yes, though Theo is in England at the moment. He was wounded at Albuera in May and has been in the military hospital in London since arriving back in England. I stayed at our town house for a few weeks, just to be near him, but he insisted that I return home. He is so independent. He never did like anyone to comfort him when he was ill, not even as a boy. Oh, the scrapes he used to get into!'

Her eyes twinkled as she regarded Lucy's interest. 'I expect you have heard about many of them. The whole county was privy to his escapades, I fear. But, he was never a *bad* boy, simply full of fun and determined to enjoy life ... and Con, of course, followed his lead.'

Her face saddened for a moment. 'I sometimes wish those days were still here. It is so hard to know one's sons are fighting on foreign battlefields and fearing they will be killed. But, I am not the only mother who suffers thus and I am thankful Theo was not fatally wounded. However, enough of that. Others are not so fortunate so I mustn't complain, even though he will be returning soon to rejoin his regiment.'

She paused as the main course covers were removed and a dish of hothouse peaches was carried in, accompanied by a bowl of freshly whipped cream. When both had been served and were enjoying the juicy fruits, Lady Montcliffe eventually asked, 'Now, how are we to occupy you on your visit? You are welcome to come and sit with me any afternoon ... and the dowager countess extends a similar invitation. However, neither of us expects you to be confined to the house or to our saloons. Do you play the pianoforte?'

'Yes, I enjoy playing music, ma'am, though I am not sure how accomplished I am,' Lucy replied modestly.

Lady Montcliffe smiled. 'I am sure you will be perfectly accomplished to play for the dowager countess and myself, if you will not find that too tiresome. I'm afraid I am at present out of touch with any young society. My health isn't what it was ... and, with the worry of my sons being in constant danger and my mother-in-law's advanced age, we live very quietly here. Though I am sure I may be able to organize a small private party for you, where you could do some dancing. Do you like to dance? I am sure young ladies like yourself enjoy dancing lessons. I know I did! Ah, those were the days, We thought they would last for ever, but, alas, they don't.'

Her gentle smile took away any sense of self-pity for the lost years of youth, but the memories of her own dancing lessons brought a blush to Lucy's cheeks and she hoped the countess didn't know of the reason for her temporary exile from home, nor her parents' order to her sister that she was *not* to be allowed to dance during her visit. 'Yes, my lady, I do like to dance but I will not pine away if I am compelled not to have the opportunity to do so for a while. I have brought some embroidery with me. I am fashioning some motifs on a layette for my new niece or nephew.' She paused and then asked hopefully, 'I also like riding. May I ride sometimes?'

'Yes, of course. I, too, enjoy riding, so we may ride out together sometimes. And we can go on carriage drives, too. I am going to enjoy your visit, Lucy. I love my sons and wouldn't change them for the world but, for a few weeks, you must indulge me and be the daughter I was never fortunate enough to have.'

At that very moment, the Earl of Montcliffe, known as Lord Rockhaven, or simply Rockhaven by his associates, and Theo by his family and friends, was stepping from his carriage and ascending the steps of the Montcliffe town house in Park Lane, Mayfair. He had been discharged from hospital earlier that day and had spent a couple of pleasant hours at his gentlemen's club before summoning his carriage. He winced as he attempted to bound up the steps, ruefully acknowledging that the wound in his side was not yet fully healed.

Never mind – he was alive! Maybe the curse upon his family had ended at last? Death had reached out to him, but he had evaded its clutches ... for now, at least!

The door opened as he reached the top step and Lord Rockhaven strode through, tossing his hat with his gloves tucked inside to Dalton, the butler.

'Welcome home, m'lord,' Dalton murmured, catching the hat with a practised hand. 'Your lady mother will be happy to know you are out of hospital at last.'

Rockhaven's steps paused. 'Er, yes. She will, of course ... though I am not returning to Montcliffe Hall just yet. A couple of weeks in Town, perhaps to ... er, build up my strength a bit; a few rounds at Jackson's, a bit of sword practice.'

Theo wondered why he felt compelled to explain himself to his butler. Guilty conscience, perhaps? He knew his mother would be disappointed when she learned of his delay in Town, but what was a chap to do? Life in a military hospital was not much different from the disciplined life on the field.

But it was he who had insisted on joining the army. As the elder son, he could have evaded the duty with no loss of valour, but that wasn't Theo's way. If he were going to die young, it may as well be on a battlefield as anywhere else. For King and country, he and Con had decided, with the arrogant confidence of youth.

But the war had robbed him and many other young men of their carefree years and he was young enough to want to seize the opportunity for some Town living whilst he could … some gaming, drinking, trips to the theatre and, perhaps, who knew, some light-hearted feminine company? Nothing serious, of course. A soldier's life was too uncertain for that.

'I might even still be here when the House resumes its autumn sitting,' he added, attempting to give some sobriety to his desire to remain in London.

'Of course,' Dalton agreed. 'It's good to have you back, m'lord.'

Theo resumed his way upstairs, whistling tunelessly, his mind already contemplating the possible delights of the evening's entertainments.

Three

IT WAS AFTER luncheon the following day when Lucy made her first visit to the dowager countess's rooms. She changed out of her morning dress, which had been suitable for a turn around the garden, into a more elaborate gown of pale-blue twilled French silk that had a pretty heart-shaped neckline and small puffed sleeves.

The dowager countess's suite of rooms was light and airy, with exquisite furniture and furnishings in shades of dusky pink, cream and gold. Lucy sank into a low curtsy, only rising when the dowager's frail voice bade her, 'Come here, child. Let me see you more clearly.'

The dowager was reclining on a day bed, her back supported by an array of cushions. She gestured a hand towards a low chair that was placed conveniently close and scrutinized Lucy's face through her lorgnette.

'Ha! And what misdemeanour were you guilty of committing, eh, miss?' the elderly lady finally barked.

'I … er … I fell in love with my dance master,' Lucy stammered, unnerved by the directness of the question, swiftly deciding that the old lady would instantly detect any prevaricating.

'Ha! Thought as much.' The dowager's eyes glimmered

with satisfaction. 'Though what's the surprise in that, I'd like to know? Society restricts young women to the company of single men of their own class and then flings totally unsuitable ones at their feet. I'll tell you a secret, shall I? At your age, I fell in love at least twice a week. My dancing master, music master, French tutor, riding master … I fell in love with the lot!'

Lucy was speechless and her wide-eyed stare betrayed the fact.

The dowager again eyed Lucy through her lorgnette. 'That surprises you, doesn't it? Though why it should, I don't know. D'you think falling in love is the prerogative of the present young generation? Hey? Cat got your tongue, has it?'

'N … no, my lady. I'm just surprised by your openness. My mother was apoplectic when she discovered my … my preference.'

'And so she should be! That's what mothers are for. What did you expect, eh? A bouquet of roses?'

'No, I just thought she might understand … after all, she loves my father.'

'Ha! Totally different. The thing is, miss, it's all right falling in love with these men, but never tell 'em so. It doesn't do. Totally unsuitable, after all! It would never be allowed. No, your mistake, I think, was telling the man and then letting your parents think you were serious.'

'Oh!' Lucy felt deflated. 'The thing is, I *was* serious. I thought he loved me, too. How could he lie so?'

'Hmm! Cutting a sham, was he? Dishing out the flummery?' The dowager eyed Lucy with a glint of mischief, as if daring her young companion to be shocked at her knowledge of some of the language of the lower classes.

Lucy didn't rise to the bait. Instead, she sighed wryly. 'And I was green enough to believe him.'

'No shame in that, girl. A show of innocence in a young girl is no bad thing as long as you learn from the experience. Think you have, eh?'

Lucy nodded sadly. 'Yes. I won't be quite so trusting again. But how will I *ever* know if someone really loves me, or simply wants to get his hands on my fortune ... for I shall never marry without true love?'

'Experience, my dear, experience. A commodity in short supply in young people. But, it will come. Give yourself time and don't take the young men you will meet during your Season too seriously. Keep them guessing. A pretty girl like you will have lots of young men paying you court. If I'm not mistaken, you'll have the whole lot of 'em falling at your feet!'

'Yes, I probably will, won't I?' Lucy laughed, accepting the truth of the statement with no thought of conceit. 'But I can't imagine falling in love again. It ... hurts too much when they let you down.'

'Ah, there's no heartache like that of your first lost love, but I suspect this one will fade with time. And, when it's the real one for you, you'll know.' Her eyes became dreamy as she added, 'I still remember the moment I first saw my Richard. I knew at once he was the one I would marry. Ha! He didn't stand a chance! Though I kept him dangling for a while before I relented and allowed him to approach my father.'

Lucy smiled at the old lady's gleeful reminiscences, finding it difficult to imagine someone so elderly as a young woman of similar age to herself. She nodded in agreement.

'Then that is what I shall do – I shall keep them guessing and then probably marry none of them!'

'That's the spirit, Miss Templeton.' The dowager laughed, nodding in approval. 'You'll do, Miss Templeton, you'll do!' She looked at Lucy thoughtfully. 'How long did you say you were staying here?'

'Just a few weeks, until my nephew and niece recover from chickenpox ... then I will return to Glenbury Lodge.'

'Mmm! Well, come and visit me again, girl, won't you? I like your spirit.'

Lucy's days at Montcliffe Hall passed swiftly and pleas-antly. In the mornings, if the weather was fine, she invariably went riding in the surrounding countryside, sometimes accompanied by Lady Montcliffe and at other times by a groom. On some afternoons the two ladies went for a carriage drive and, on one lovely day, visited nearby Ely Cathedral. Other afternoons, she sat with either of the two countesses, sometimes playing the pianoforte or reading aloud to them, or quietly stitching and enjoying light conversation. And, in the evenings, she often went to the library to choose a book to read either in the sitting-room or upstairs in her bedroom.

Susie kept her up-to-date with any servants' gossip and excitedly passed on to her mistress mention of the 'Rockhaven curse' that had bedevilled former generations of the family. Lucy was intrigued. She cast back her mind, remembering that Marissa had once made a comment about the family's tragic history, though any tentative enquiries had been met with shaken heads and pursed lips.

Her chance to discover more came one afternoon when she

was sitting with the dowager countess. She had read a few pages of *A Comedy Of Errors* from Charles and Mary Lamb's *Tales From Shakespeare*, but had ceased when the old lady's head began to drop to her chest. Just when Lucy was about to creep away, the dowager revived and resumed her favourite topic of asking Lucy about her interests and about her social life now that she was out of the schoolroom, comparing it with her own life at a similar age. Her many questions emboldened Lucy to try a bit of direct questioning herself.

'My lady, may I ask *you* a question ... a personal one?'

The dowager took her time in answering, but then nodded. 'You may ask, but I might not give you an answer.'

'It's about your family, my lady. Why do people say your family is under a curse?'

'Ha! You don't pull your punches, do you, miss?'

Lucy was instantly apologetic. 'I'm sorry, my lady, it was impertinent of me. Please forgive me.'

'No, no! I asked you questions just as impertinent. If you can't take it, don't give it, I always say. So, the Rockhaven curse, eh? Hmmph, I'm glad you asked *me*, rather than gossiping with the servants. Well, the *curse*, my dear, is that the firstborn son of the past three generations of the Rockhaven family has died young – though each was considerate enough to evade his demise until he had sired an heir. My father-in-law died of alcoholic poisoning; my husband died in a duel; and my son died in a driving accident. He was forever out to cut a dash. Hunting the squirrel, is what they call it: the practice of following behind a carriage and then passing it so tightly that they brush the wheels. My son brushed the wheel too closely and his carriage overturned.'

Lucy looked puzzled. She hesitated, trying to find the right words to best express her thoughts. 'I'm sorry to hear your family have suffered that heartache three times in three generations, but surely it is only superstition to think it of it as a curse. After all, a hard drinker will inevitably die of alcoholic poisoning and a reckless driver of an accident.'

'Exactly! There is no common connection among the three early deaths, so, there is no logical reason to suppose that Theodore will suffer an early demise in some spectacular way, is there?'

'No reason at all, my lady,' Lucy replied lightly. 'Does he expect such an early demise?'

'It wouldn't surprise me, child. Every childhood spill or minor injury he suffered caused the gossips to repeat the nonsense. Say a thing often enough and people begin to believe it! I always hoped Theo would be too level-headed to let it blight his life, but the wildness of his past behaviour, aided and abetted by his wretched cousin, and his current occupation on the Peninsular doesn't exactly compel me to hope too much.'

Lucy's interest was roused. 'His cousin? I haven't heard mention of a cousin.'

'Aye, Piers Potterill. A cousin twice removed, but next in line for the title after Conrad. Never liked him! I always suspected him of goading the boys on, and neither would ever refuse a challenge. Too much like their father and grandfather for their own good!'

The old lady suddenly leaned forward, her eyes bright.

'Tell me, Miss Templeton, would *you* consider becoming the wife of my grandson Theodore, the present Earl of Montcliffe?'

Lucy stared at the dowager countess in some consternation, not wanting to upset the old lady by an outright refusal.

'Why … no. No! I do not even know him. I told you, I will not marry without love.'

The elderly lady laughed drily, though her eyes glinted with mischief. 'So you did, my dear. So you did!' She nodded her head several times, as if in agreement with Lucy's words. Then her animation faded and her expression saddened. 'But I asked the question hypothetically really, Miss Templeton. By "you", I really mean "anybody" … any attractive young woman with a degree of intelligent caution in her, that is. You supplied the answer. And that, to *my* mind, is the Rockhaven curse.'

'You fear that he will never marry and your family line will die out? But surely some women would agree to marry him simply for the title.'

'Possibly but most families hope to see their line continued. It would take an insensitive parent to inflict such a heartache on their daughter. Ah well! Maybe you will meet Theo one day and change your mind.'

Lucy shook her head. 'I don't think so, my lady. Once I have made up my mind about something, I invariably try to keep to it. Mama says I have a stubborn streak.'

'Does she indeed! Well, so have I. However, I am tired now, so run along, Miss Templeton. I'm sure there are many other things you would rather do with your time than listen to an old lady like me rambling on.'

Lucy made her curtsy and withdrew, reflectively pondering the bad hand of fate that had been dealt to the Rockhaven line.

*

However, much as she was enjoying her stay at Montcliffe Hall, after four weeks Lucy began to hope that her visit might be curtailed very soon. Her natural lively disposition had little outlet and the summer days were beginning to seem wearisome.

Her departure became imminent a few days later, when a letter was delivered telling Lady Montcliffe that Dr Walmsley had declared the Glenbury Lodge nursery at last clear of the chickenpox and that her young guest was able to be restored to the bosom of her family. To mark Lucy's last evening with them, the dowager countess was carried downstairs to join Lady Montcliffe and Lucy in the dining room.

Susie insisted on putting out Lucy's finest evening gown – a delightful creation of patterned pale-lemon crepe trimmed with festoons of silk, tied at the high waist with a contrasting satin bow, the ends of which fell down her back. It had a modest neckline, trimmed with lace-edged scallops of the same material and its tiny puffed sleeves finished with the same lace edging. Susie then fashioned Lucy's hair into a knot on the crown of her head, decorated with tiny flowers fresh from the garden.

After the three ladies had partaken of their meal, the two older ladies made their apologies and retired to their apartments upstairs, leaving Lucy to her own devices. A glimpse of the rose garden, still bathed in the evening sunshine, attracted her attention.

'I know you have a lot of packing to do,' she told Susie, when she went upstairs to collect a light shawl. 'So, I think I will take a short turn about the garden.'

'Eeh, not on your own, Miss Lucy!' Susie objected. 'I can do the packing later.'

'Nonsense, Susie! What possible harm can befall me in Lady Montcliffe's garden? No, you continue with the packing up here and I promise to return before the sun has sunk below the line of trees.'

It was a balmy evening. The scent of the flowers floated in the air and Lucy breathed them in deeply. She had enjoyed her stay at Montcliffe Hall but, although sorry to be leaving the two countesses, she was now looking forward to returning to Glenbury Lodge to spend some time with her nephew and niece and helping them through their convalescence. With a burst of carefree abandon, no doubt caused by her deep inhalation of the heady scents of the flowers, she flung wide her arms and danced and twirled among the flowerbeds, by some chance humming the music of the waltz that had led to her deportation from her home. How often had she imagined dancing it with Mario Vitali in the early days of her exile?

She was now surprised to find that the memory no longer distressed her. In fact, she was able to dismiss any thought of the wretched man as easily as she might have swatted away an irritating midge on a summer evening. She had come to realize that her love for Signor Vitali had been nothing more than the illusion of a young girl's infatuation – blatantly fostered by a heartless fortune hunter – and the agony of betrayal was fading, leaving her wiser than she had been before. It had left her determined not to be swept into a relationship against her will. She would be the mistress of her destiny … no one else, not even her parents.

Pushing such serious thoughts away from her, she twirled and swayed, letting her feet take her where they wished, her mind lost in the steady rhythmic beat of the waltz. Her steps took her to the flagged area outside the music room, the way she had left the hall. There she twirled and stepped some more, her head thrown back into the falling rays of the sun as it began its descent towards the distant trees that bordered the grounds.

The sound of slow clapping forced its way into her consciousness and her steps faltered to a halt as her eyes searched for the source of the sound. She felt a little alarmed to see the figure of a young man leaning against the open glass doors. He was well dressed but seemed to be more than slightly dishevelled. Her alarm grew as the man lurched forward, murmuring, 'Well, well, well, and who have we here?'

Lucy backed away as the man advanced towards her. She wasn't greatly alarmed for her safety as she now recognized the man's features from the oil painting that adorned the dining room wall. It was the elder of the two sons of the house – Lord Theodore Rockhaven – but his unsteady progress towards her clearly demonstrated that he was in his cups. 'As drunk as a lord!' Lucy couldn't help reflecting, with a slightly hysterical hiccup.

Even in the fading light, she could see that his eyelids drooped slightly over his deep-brown eyes, giving him an unnerving Machiavellian demeanour. Her heart palpitated and she held out her hand, palm forward, in the hope of fending the man away from her, but, instead, her hand was seized and used to draw her towards her captive against the young man's chest.

'Sir, I implore you!' she gasped in dismay.

Lord Rockhaven laughed, his white teeth gleaming in the fading light. 'Impl … plore me?' he drawled with exaggerated carefulness, his brandy-laden breath assailing her nostrils as he pulled her against his hard body, his right hand in the small of her back, holding her close. 'Hap … happy to oblige, m'dear!'

Lucy opened her mouth to protest against such unseemly handling of her but, before any words were spoken, she felt his warm lips cover hers and move upon them in a fashion that both repelled and excited her at the same time. The alcoholic fumes seemed to make her head dizzy, but there was a surprising gentleness about the action that sent a strange sensation spiralling around her body – a sensation that turned her insides to a flaming fire and her legs to jelly, causing her momentarily to lean against him. For a brief moment she felt perfectly safe in his embrace – then sanity returned and she tried to twist her head away but could not. As he firmly forced her lips apart and his tongue began to caress hers, she felt the strangest of sensations begin to stir in the pit of her stomach.

She recognized the sensations as similar to those she had only a few weeks earlier experienced in the arms of her dance-master – only more intense – and, for a moment, she allowed the sweet spiralling of desire to sweep around her body, lost in wonder at the dizzying experience. The man groaned softly, startling Lucy back to reality. What was she doing, responding in this way to a drunken man? A response she knew to be totally unbefitting that of a well-brought up young lady! He might be the son of her hostess but, to her, he was a stranger and, at this moment, a most unwelcome one!

Lord Rockhaven's lips began to trace the line of her jaw and down her throat, generating a surge of alarm in Lucy's heart. She suddenly felt repelled by the intimacy of what was happening and, from melting compliance, she transformed into fiery resistance. How dare he treat her so? Desperately, she began to struggle to free herself. At first, her struggles seemed to enflame the passion of her attacker – for that is how it now felt. An assault upon her body and virtue.

As she persisted in her struggles, Lord Rockhaven swayed sideways a little and Lucy immediately took advantage by pushing strongly against his chest. Although she was a much slighter figure, her head wasn't befuddled by drink and, feeling his hold on her slacken, she quickly stepped backwards, swinging her right hand against his cheek as she did so.

In any other circumstances, Lord Rockhaven's startled expression might have amused her, but she was now too incensed by his ungentlemanly behaviour to find any part of his assault upon her in the slightest degree amusing.

'Vixen!' Lord Rockhaven growled, instantly letting go of her. His left hand tenderly touched his cheek, but Lucy felt no inclination to apologize for her action. The man deserved all she had given him – and more. But not from her. Not now.

Realizing that she was now free of his hold, she gathered up the hem of her gown and darted away from him through the open French windows and through the music room.

Lord Rockhaven made no real attempt to follow her. Indeed, his swaying figure was incapable of doing so. He belatedly staggered a few steps in her wake and then thankfully took hold of the framework of the glass doors. He was unclear what had happened, or, indeed, if anything had happened at all. The delicately pirouetting beauty had surely been a figment of his imagination, except his left cheek still stung and he tenderly touched it once more.

He knew he was as drunk as a wheelbarrow. Since hearing three days ago of the death of his commanding officer and others in his regiment, he had been dipping far too deeply. It had seemed the only way to cope with those particular deaths and all the others announced daily in the *London Gazette* – men he knew personally, or rather *had* known, his befuddled mind corrected itself. He should have simply returned to the Peninsular without coming to call on his mama and grandmother incurring their disappointment in that way, rather than the distress they would feel to see him thus incapacitated.

The sound of hurrying footsteps penetrated his befuddled mind.

'Crawford!' he murmured, and slowly crumpled down the framework of the door until he lay sprawled at his manservant's feet.

Lucy hurried upstairs, her breath ragged with the unaccustomed excitement and enforced exertion. She had the presence of mind to pause as she had reached the upper landing and peer over the balustrade. There was no sound of pursuit. She took a few deep breaths and slowly exhaled, sensing that her heartbeat was returning to normal. Deep within, her heart was at war with itself, partly exulting in the memory of the dizzying desire she had felt and partly ashamed of her fleeting compliance. She lightly touched her lips with the tips of her fingers, wondering if she would ever feel that surge of overwhelming desire with another man. She knew that anything less would never satisfy her now!

The following day, Lucy was awakened by the swish of her bedroom curtains being drawn back, flooding her room with light. As she screwed her eyes against the bright sunlight, her maid excitedly announced that the young master had returned home late the previous evening but, due to a number of wounds he had received in the course of his military action on the Peninsular, he needed a time of recuperation and was to be secluded in his rooms for this day at least.

'Hmm!' Lucy couldn't help reflecting wryly. 'The ideal remedy for a hangover!'

Not that she gave any indication of her private assessment of Lord Rockhaven's state of health when she made her farewells to the countess and dowager countess later in the morning. The countess was clearly delighted by her elder son's return.

'All I need now is to see Conrad also,' she said passionately.

The dowager was more outspoken. 'Hmm! Pity you are leaving us today, Miss Templeton.' Her pale eyes gleamed mischievously. 'You could always delay your departure for a couple of days. I could claim that I needed your presence, eh? Give you an opportunity to meet my wayward grandson?'

Lucy smiled at her blatant attempt at matchmaking. 'I think not, my lady. Besides, I am told that seventeen is too young to know my own mind with regard to matrimony.'

'Not even to make an old lady happy?'

Lucy shook her head. 'No, ma'am.'

'Ah well. I won't give up complete hope; after all, he must find himself a wife sometime soon … if he can! Maybe his mama will persuade him to leave the army and look over next Season's marriage mart? The right person might curb his wildness. You *will* be there, will you not?'

Lucy remembered the disturbing feel of Lord Rockhaven's lips upon her own, but he was obviously a man of loose morals and she had no wish to fall prey to his advances.

'Yes, my lady, but I do not intend to set my cap at any young man, let alone one whose reputation is as colourful as your grandson's.'

'Unless you fall in love with him?'

Lucy smiled at the old lady's persistence. 'That is highly unlikely, ma'am.'

'Maybe so. Off you go, then. It's been a pleasure knowing you, Miss Templeton.'

'And you, ma'am.'

She leaned over the old lady and kissed her papery-thin cheek. She sensed she might never see her again.

Four

LUCY WAS LOOKING forward to spending some time with her young nephew and niece, but the children's nurse allowed her very little access to the children under the excuse that they were convalescent and must be kept quiet, though Lucy couldn't help suspecting that Nurse Harvey was more concerned about the effect their young aunt's sullied reputation might have upon their character.

Consequently, life was tedious and dull. Since Marissa was now in the third trimester, her thoughts were becoming more focused on her approaching confinement. She had temporarily retired from society and received only married ladies from the local area into her drawing room and was content to recline on a *chaise-longue* for such times of the day when she had only Lucy for company.

Lucy threw herself wholeheartedly into being a companion to her sister, though there were times when her fingers gently touched her lips and she would find herself recalling the sensations that had swirled around her, melting her insides to liquid fire, as the earl's lips had ravaged hers. Then she would impatiently snatch her fingers away and indignantly chastise herself for giving way to such wayward thoughts. His drunken behaviour ought to have repelled her – indeed it *did* – but something about him had also excited her.

It wasn't the same as the excitement Mario's clandestine love-making had created. In one sense, it was more physical than that and had stirred strange longings that Lucy didn't fully understand and for which she instantly berated herself. Hadn't she learned her lesson from her foolish adoration of her dancing master? Was she destined to flutter from one infatuation to another, making a moon-cake out of herself, a source of amusement to those around her? Indeed, she hoped not!

In fact, she would wager that her tender thoughts were influenced by the dowager countess's fondness for her grandson. But, there was something about his eyes that lingered in her memory. There seemed to be a sadness lurking behind the half-hooded expression. A sadness that seemed to reach out to her in appeal, but an appeal for what? What interest would a hardened rake have in an inexperienced girl like herself? She didn't know. All she knew was that she had felt there was some sort of vulnera-bility about him – a vulnerability that would normally be hidden under a more dashing exterior.

Huh! Was she foolish enough to think that she could 'save him from himself'? Did she hope to show him that the curse that had seemed to beleaguer the family had no control over him unless he let it?

Whatever it was, she felt confused by the strange power that those few moments in his embrace had over her. However, she wasn't going to confide any of her confusion to her sister. Good heavens! Were she to do so, she would be banished to a convent, or some such outlandish place.

Locked away and guarded day and night. And she would have to say goodbye to her Season in London before it even began. No, no, no! She mustn't confide in Marissa. If her weeks of banishment had taught her anything, it was to enjoy her Season to its utmost, and she fully intended to follow the dowager's advice with regard to any young dandy who fancied his chance with her ... unless, of course, one managed to stir her heart!

However, Lucy's frequent lapses into a dream-like state did not go unnoticed by her sister, though Marissa mistook the instigator of her sister's preoccupation.

'You must cast Signor Vitali out of your mind, Lucy dear,' she admonished her. 'He behaved despicably, and it is of no use to moon about looking so Friday-faced wishing you were at home. Mama sent you here for a time to reflect on your foolish behaviour – not to be enjoying a round of outings and parties with other young people. You should read some character improving books – I'm sure Mama will approve – and you should continue to embroider the layette you started. I'm surprised you didn't finish it whilst you were at Montcliffe Hall. I'm sure there was ample opportunity.'

'I did do some stitching,' Lucy defended herself, 'but I spent most of each afternoon reading to both Lady Montcliffe and the dowager countess and, some days, I accompanied Lady Montcliffe on a gentle ride within their estate.'

'Hmm, well, all I can say is that I sent for you not a moment too soon, for I hear the Earl of Montcliffe is back home.' She looked at Lucy's face suspiciously, which Lucy knew had turned a little pink at Marissa's mention of the

Earl. 'At least, I *hope* you removed from there in time. It wouldn't do for you to have remained at Montcliffe Hall with such a man of wild character in residence, even if his mother was there to chaperon you. You *didn't* meet him, did you?'

Lucy felt her heart skip a beat, knowing that it would be extreme foolishness to confess her unfortunate encounter with the Earl of Montcliffe to Marissa. Her sister had never looked at another man other than The Hon. Rupert Cunningham. She would be scandalized by such a revelation and would doubtless feel compelled to pass on such shocking news to their mama.

Lucy tried to marshal her thoughts. 'The earl … er … arrived late on my last evening at Montcliffe Hall, quite some time after dinner. Both Lady Montcliffe and the dowager retire early, you know, and I was in the habit of taking a book up to my room,' Lucy replied quite truthfully, whilst evading a direct answer to Marissa's question. 'When Susie awoke me in the morning, she had learned from the kitchen staff that the earl is still recovering from the wounds he received at Albuera and was to be confined to his own suite of rooms for the time being. Your carriage arrived for me long before any part of his retinue made any appearance downstairs.'

'Thank goodness for that,' Marissa breathed, fanning her face with her hand. 'I dread to think what Mama would have said had circumstances turned out otherwise!'

And Lucy sighed with relief, knowing that her second slip from propriety would remain her secret forever. The encounter had changed her. She now recognized that there were different depths of feeling and that cupid's darts could strike from unexpected sources, bringing torment as well as well as fulfilment of joy.

She welcomed the brief opportunity of near solitude to mull over her new understanding, and her remaining days at Glenbury Lodge were filled with the ladylike pursuits of reading, stitching, playing a few of Marissa's favourite tunes on the pianoforte. Only when Bertie and Arabella were brought to spend a short time with their mother before going to bed was she able to forget that she was there under a cloud and play some quiet childhood games with her nephew and niece.

However, it was quite a relief when, in mid-October, her mama decided that her exile had been long enough to leave a lasting impression upon her and sent the carriage to take her home. Lady Templeton threw herself into the delightful delirium of organizing her younger daughter's extensive wardrobe of clothes that would be essential for her to be adequately attired in order to stand out from all the other hopeful debutantes in the approaching London Season.

From the beginning of November until mid-January, with barely a break for the festivities of Christmas, Lady Templeton's favourite modistes, accompanied by a train of footmen bearing rolls of fine cloth for a bevy of seam-stresses to stitch, flooded in an endless stream through the upper rooms of the Templeton home. Milliners brought boxes and boxes of hats and bonnets, each to be fashioned and trimmed with net and sprigs of flowers and feathers, perfectly matched to the many gowns. Haberdashers brought their numerous wares: stockings of silk of various hues decorated with clocks of many designs; scarves, bags, fans and muffs ... far more than Lucy could imagine one person could wear in two whole years, let alone the months from late January until July.

Within six weeks, Lucy found herself in possession of numerous day dresses for walking and promenading; more dresses for afternoon wear, for giving or receiving visits, for riding in a carriage or on horseback and a vast number of low-cut evening dresses and ball gowns.

The crowning glory of her entire new wardrobe was the magnificent gown for her presentation at court, the tradition that launched the young ladies of upper-class families into Society.

It was during this time that a black-edged letter was delivered to Glenbury Lodge. Marissa's heart was all of a flutter until Rupert had opened the letter and declared that his dear wife need not worry. The communiqué did not contain dire news about either of her parents or sister, but contained the sad news of Dowager Countess Montcliffe's demise. Condolences were sent to the family, who were now in full mourning.

When the letter was forwarded to Lord and Lady Templeton in London, Lucy was indeed heartily sorry at the sad tidings, for she had liked the old lady. At least, she reflected, she need not now fear that Lord Rockhaven's presence might mar her first Season in London, but, if she were honest, she also felt a degree of disappointment. Would he have recognized her? She doubted it. He probably had no memory at all of his unchivalrous behaviour towards her!

The Season was a non-stop round of parties, assemblies, routs and balls with the many hostesses vying with each other to have hosted the best 'crush' of the Season. Along with many other dazzling but nervous debutantes, Lucy was presented at court and, thereafter, received vouchers for the weekly assemblies at Almacks. It wasn't Lucy's favourite venue for balls and she secretly thought its décor to be less grand and far more stuffy than she had expected.

That disappointment was more than made up for by visits to the theatres, museums and art galleries and other such delights of London, and carriage drives in Hyde Park, where the dandies strutted and the ladies sashayed and simpered, coyly casting down their eyes when the gentlemen flattered and complimented them.

Lucy was immensely popular and it was very gratifying to be paid exuberant compliments by the bucks and beaux, even if they did seem to be a little immature in their demeanour and behaviour. She was never short of admirers; invitations to events were delivered to the house every day; so many that she was obliged to refuse more than half of them and often attended as many as three events in one evening, so as not to offend the many influential hostesses. Her dance card was filled within half an hour of arriving at any ball and it could be as late as two or three in the morning when her maid helped divest her of her evening clothes and drew back the covers of her bed so that Lucy could collapse into instant sleep.

She loved the excitement and constant activity of the social life and lived it to the full, but there were many of the accepted customs and behaviour of the *ton* that she secretly despised. The rules and regulations were so false, a mere coating of respectability and correct behaviour; the points of etiquette so complex that it was like a maze that could bewilder and trip the unwary. Lucy inadvertently flouted many restrictions placed upon the young ladies. Some of the more modest debutantes looked askance when she rode in Hyde Park with her many admirers, even though she was accompanied by a groom. And eyebrows were raised when she took the reins of an escort's carriage when offered the opportunity, an action which endeared her to the admiring bucks, who were often overheard to be describing her as 'an out and outer', a 'prime article' and being 'bang up to the mark'!

Her mama lived in constant dread of her daughter being labelled a 'hoyden' or being 'fast'. But Lucy's natural cheerfulness and lack of guile saved her from being condemned by the rival mamas – that and the growing realization that the vivacious Miss Templeton was turning down the offers of marriage that she received from the bucks who were so bold as to make their offers early in the Season.

At first, her mama was in agreement. 'You can do far better than him,' she murmured when a deflated younger son of a baronet took his leave. 'I sometimes think I was too hasty in accepting your papa. I might have landed an earl if I had held out a while longer.'

Even when Lucy declined an advantageous offer from a middle-aged viscount, her mama's censure was only brief and half-hearted, but when Lucy refused to even *hear* an offer from the second son of the Earl of Standish, her condemnation was more stringent. 'You will do as I say, Lucy! You can expect no better an offer than this. Your papa will be most annoyed if you are not settled by the end of the Season. He will not be so tolerant as to allow you another, you know.'

'But I do not love him, Mama.'

'Pah! What has love to do with marriage? He is tolerably likeable and extremely wealthy. You would want for nothing!'

'But I do not wish to be married to someone for whom I have no affection, Mama.'

'But what will become of you, Lucy?' Lady Templeton responded. 'What can a woman from our station in life do except be married and fill her husband's nursery?'

'She can remain single and have charge of her own life,' Lucy replied spiritedly.

'Not with the sanction of Society! Oh, why can't you be like Marissa, who accepted the first man of standing who offered for her?'

But Lucy was *not* like her sister and made no pretence of being so. If she had been more like her sister, there is no doubt that she would not have begged her mama to accept an invitation to a private masquerade party at Vauxhall Gardens, but all that she had heard about it made it seem like an exciting, intriguing place of entertainment. Her friends all agreed.

'And surely Lady Birchley wouldn't hold a private party in a place that is unsuitable for young people!' she pushed her case. 'After all, her own granddaughter, Lady Sophie, is to attend and absolutely everyone who is of note will be there. Please, Mama!'

Lady Templeton finally agreed. After all, if the majority of the social elite were to be there, who knows who might spot her daughter and be taken by her.

'Very well, Lucy. But you must stay close to me and the others of our party. On no account must you wander off without a chaperon, for you must be aware that the Gardens are open to the general public and anyone who can afford the entrance fee of three shillings is likely to be there!' A slight shudder accompanied the final part of her warning and Lucy suppressed a wry smile at her mother's fine sense of social superiority.

'Oh, thank you, Mama! It will be a most wonderful evening. May I send a note round to Eliza to tell her that we are to attend?'

That done, Lucy immediately repaired to her room to seek Susie's help in choosing what she would wear. Over the next few days, the masquerade party at Vauxhall was the main topic of conversation among the young people, especially regarding their dress. Lucy eventually chose a pale-pink muslin gown with a dusky pink silk pelisse and matching domino.

Early in the evening, the party assembled at Lady Birchley's town residence and drove in convoy to the landing stage opposite to Vauxhall Gardens, which stood on the south bank of the Thames near Lambeth. They crossed the Thames by boat and passed through the water entrance to be immediately entranced by the thousands of lanterns that hung in festoons from the branches of the trees that lined the promenades. The lights twinkled like stars and were reflected in the sparkling water of the magnificent fountains that danced and splashed around the grounds, set among artificial ruins and magnificent tableaux.

The party made a colourful sight, the hooded Venetian cloaks of the ladies offset by the darker hues worn by the gentlemen. The fact that everyone was masked added to the gaiety and excitement and many otherwise well-behaved young ladies indulged in a degree of mild flirting that would have been unthought of without the anonymity of their dress, a ploy that Lucy immediately thought to be quite superfluous, as most disguises were rendered ineffectual when the wearers spoke. Why, anyone could tell that the Elizabethan courtier was Harry Crawthorne and that the elaborate, many caped silver costume covered no other than Robert Harrington! But, no matter, the young men were well-schooled by their mamas and tutors and extravagant compliments and clever ripostes were tossed about and received with good humour and varying degrees of delight, depending on who had made the compliment and to whom it was directed. It was all part of the courting game that was part of the Season.

Many of the revellers in other groups or parties were also wearing masked dominoes, which engendered much amusement, as wild guesses were made as to the identities thus concealed or disguised. 'Even the Prince Regent and his cohorts come here,' one knowledgeable young man informed the group. 'Why, that masked Tudor courtier over there, no doubt intending to resemble King Henry VIII, might well be he!'

'I doubt it,' another remarked drily. 'His Royal Highness would need three such costumes to cover his ample figure!'

An orchestra gave a two-part concert in the rotunda every evening at eight o'clock and, after listening to the performance, Lady Birchley's party strolled in groups along the pathways, chattering and laughing and enjoying the fun and excitement of being in a group of exuberant young people.

There was so much to excite their senses. Famous

singers, actors and actresses performed in decorated booths and jugglers and illusionists performed their acts. The evening sped by and in no time at all, it seemed, they were gathering together for supper, held in a number of supper-boxes that Lady Birchley had hired for her party. Each one held six or eight people and waiters served delicious slivers of ham or chicken and exotic salads. The older revellers drank burnt-wine or sampled the famous arrack-punch, which was far too strong for the younger revellers, who were guided to the selections of ratafia and light punches.

Supper was just over when a burst of golden sparks lit the darkened sky.

'Oh, the fireworks are starting!' Lucy's friend Eliza exclaimed. 'Do come, Lucy!' She grabbed hold of Lucy's hand. 'We'll see them much better in the open.'

The two girls, followed by others, hurried down the steps and were soon caught up in a throng of people jostling for better positions to see the fireworks display. Every time a new cascade of shining stars illuminated the sky, gasps of 'Ooh!' and 'Aah!' were breathed into the night air. The atmosphere was magical.

A crush of people behind Lucy pushed her forward and she lost hold of Eliza's hand. As soon as she could slip side-ways out of the press she did so and looked around for the light-blue domino of her friend, but she couldn't see her. People were still moving forward and she let them overtake her, hoping that Eliza would soon be back by her side.

The crowd was good-humoured and Lucy wasn't worried about being separated from Eliza and the others whom she knew, but, suddenly, a hand grasped her arm and a male voice hissed, 'Quick! Come this way!'

'What? Who are you?' Lucy tried to pull away and she turned to try to identify who was holding on to her.

It was a man in a black domino and only the lower part of his face was visible and that not very clear in the twilight.

Lucy couldn't remember any men of their party dressed in such a way, but maybe she was mistaken in that. She laughed a little hesitantly, trying to pull her arm free of his hold. 'Come, sir! Don't tease. We are missing the firework display.'

But when he didn't respond, pulling her instead further into the grove of trees, she began to feel alarmed. They had all been warned that pickpockets roamed the grounds looking for likely victims. Was that whom her attacker was? Was he hoping to rob her? If so, he was destined to be unlucky!

'Let go of me!' she demanded indignantly, trying to stop him pulling her deeper into the grove. 'I have no money upon my person. How dare you treat me so! Unhand me at once!'

The noise of the revellers faded, and now in a small clearing, Lucy felt herself pulled into an embrace.

'Ah, *cara mia!*' the man spoke at last. 'At last we can be together!'

Lucy froze. She remembered that voice and the Italian phrase. 'Mario?' she questioned, unable to quite believe what was happening. 'What are you *doing*? I want nothing to do with you! Let go of me at once so that I may return to my friends!'

'Ah, my leetle Lucy! How I have missed you since we were so cruelly torn apart! I have languished for you these past months! Do you not remember how you used to melt into my arms? How you used to long for me to be able to kiss you and make you my own? And now we can!'

Lucy tried to pull away. 'I remember how you demanded money from my father in return for your silence!' she cried indignantly. 'Not one word of love did you declare then!'

Mario shrugged. 'I knew it would be of no use, my leetle love. Your father was intent on separating us. But now, we have the chance to elope. I have been watching you and waiting for this chance. We can be on our way immediately. Come, my darling! My chaise is ready by Westminster Bridge. Come!'

He tried to draw her with him but when Lucy stood her ground, his voice grew impatient. 'You know it is what you have longed for. I have heard about the delightful Miss Templeton refusing all offers of marriage from some very eligible suitors.' His voice softened again, as he added, 'Ah, how I exulted to hear it. I knew you were waiting for me. What can all those young puppies hope to offer you, when you have tasted the excitement of real love?'

Lucy was speechless. She couldn't believe what she was hearing. She drew herself erect. 'Those *young puppies*, as you describe them, at least know the correct way to approach the lady of their choice! And, no, I haven't refused the offers of marriage with you in mind. I am happy to say I realized how shallow you are many months ago and I have absolutely no feelings of love left for you!' She remembered a word her father had used about this man. 'You are a charlatan, sir! Now, release me and allow me to return to my friends and ...' – her heart suddenly quailed and she began to feel the first stirrings of fear – '... and we will forget this incident ever happened.'

She heard him suck in his breath, then, 'Ah, no! That cannot be. You see, I need money and you, my little sweeting, are my means of getting it!' All traces of an Italian accent were gone and the mouth below the black mask twisted unpleasantly.

Before Lucy could react, Mario pulled her roughly to him and brutally covered her mouth with his. This was no pleasant kiss. His lips were hard and he thrust his tongue into her mouth forcefully, harshly plundering the sweetness of it. Whilst Lucy's senses were still reeling, he whirled her body around and pushed her hard against the trunk of a tree. Immediately, he thrust his knee between her legs, pinning her body between the tree and himself.

Lucy fought him. She tore the domino from his head and yanked hard at his hair. Mario responded by pulling back her hood, dislodging the pins that held her hair in place and grasping hold of her hair in both his hands. The pain brought tears to Lucy's eyes and she tried to pull his hands away. 'Help me! Someone, help me!' she cried out.

Mario immediately slapped her face, knocking her head against the tree trunk. She almost passed out and feared she would be ravished by this unprincipled man.

Through the haze that seemed to have seeped into her mind she heard a voice call out from beyond the shrubbery, 'Hello? Is anyone there?'

Mario covered her mouth with his hand but Lucy bit hard into it. As he pulled his hand away, she cried out, 'Help me! I'm being attacked!'

She heard an oath, followed by the sounds of someone forcing their way through the shrubbery towards them. She felt weak with relief. As the tension slipped out of her body,

Mario viciously thrust her aside and she felt herself falling to the ground.

'You'll be sorry for this! I'll see you ruined!' Mario snarled, and, after a vicious kick at her crumpled body, he crashed away in the opposite direction from her rescuer.

Five

IF LUCY HAD been tempted to think that her troubles were over because she had been rescued from her would-be abductor, she was soon disillusioned. Her rescuer was one of their own party who had been sent to look for her, and others were quickly upon the scene. They were shocked to find her lying crumpled on the ground with her domino torn, her gown dishevelled and dirty, and her hair tousled about her head.

Lucy tried to rise, but the pain from Mario's kick made the movement too painful and it was Viscount Hugh Wymont who lifted her up into his arms and carried her back to the path from where she had been dragged. Although he had made some attempt to tidy her gown around her, the sorry state of her person and attire was obvious to all and Lucy heard shocked gasps from some of the ladies present.

Indeed, some of the mamas in attendance hurriedly placed themselves between their daughters and the distressing sight Miss Templeton presented and ushered their daughters from the scene, but Lucy's friend Eliza pushed herself forward to reach her friend, whose limp form still draped in Lord Wymont's arms.

'Lucy! Whatever happened? One minute you were by my side and the next you were gone! I couldn't find you! Oh, my goodness!' Her eyes widened as she took in Lucy's dishevelled state. 'W-What happened?' she whispered in shocked tones.

'I ... I was attacked,' Lucy said faintly, gulping back tears that threatened to erupt. At least she had the presence of mind not to name her attacker at this point. She felt too embarrassed to have been so taken in by him the year before and was shocked by his present callous treatment of her. She felt as though she were in the midst of a nightmare and all she wanted to do was to wake up and find it had indeed been a dream. No such escape was allowed her.

Lady Templeton, having been earlier alerted by Eliza to her daughter's disappearance, arrived on the scene, her mind a mixture of anxiety at the reports of Lucy's disappearance, relief at her return, and a foreboding of the damage the incident would do to Lucy's reputation. She took immediate charge, sending one of the younger men to alert their coachman that their carriage was required forthwith and bade Viscount Wymont carry her daughter to the pick-up point. She postponed her recriminations until they were in the privacy of their home.

Lucy sobbed in her mother's arms throughout the journey and, although she managed, with some assistance, to hobble up the steps and into the house, once she was inside, she collapsed on to the tiled floor and was carried upstairs to her room by two of the footmen, who lost no time in reporting below stairs that the young mistress had been brought home in a sorry state of distress and disarray.

With tight lips, Lady Templeton ordered hot water to be brought upstairs so that Lucy could be bathed and was shocked by the bruises that were already beginning to form on Lucy's abdomen and hip.

'Who was he?' she demanded. 'Did you manage to get a good look at him?'

Lucy gulped back her tears. 'Yes,' she whispered.

'Good. We must alert the Runners. Do you think you could describe him to them?'

Lucy nodded her head faintly, knowing her answer would be of no comfort to her mother. 'It was Mario Vitali,' she whispered. 'He pulled me into the shrubbery and tried to entice me to elope with him.'

'*Elope* with him? Lucy! Whatever have you done?' Her mama's voice rose to a wail. 'How *could* you be so disobedient as to meet with that man?'

'I didn't, Mama! I didn't! He said he had been watching me and had been waiting his chance to entice me away! He thought ...' Her voice choked on the words. 'He thought I was still in love with him. But I'm not! You and Papa were right. He is a cheat and a deceiver. He isn't even Italian! Even that was false! I hate him!'

Her mother looked at her carefully. 'Lucy, you must tell me. Did he...? Did he hurt you? In a more intimate way, I mean?'

Blushing at her mama's words, Lucy shook her head. 'No ... he meant to entice me into a carriage so that we could elope. He was angry when I refused and struggled against him. He threw me to the ground and kicked me out of sheer spite. Oh, Mama, it was horrible! I don't think I shall ever trust a man again!'

Lady Templeton tightened her lips grimly. 'After tonight's episode, you may never be given the chance, Lucy. Word will get round, you know. And it will lose nothing in the telling. I'm afraid Society will shun you from now on.'

'But it wasn't my fault, Mama! I truly didn't know he would be there. It was quite by chance that Eliza and I were separated in the crush to see the fireworks … and I fought against him. I did! Nothing *really* happened!'

'In the eyes of Society it did. You have lost your inno-cence. You are tainted. Oh, if only you had accepted Edmund Standish's offer, or one of the others, this would never have happened.'

Lady Templeton's fears proved correct. Before the next day was over, gossip about the incident was already spreading. The true details were coloured with other insid-ious rumours, namely, that worse than was being admitted had befallen the unfortunate Miss Templeton. Others heard that it was an assignation gone wrong, that an elopement had been planned. Society delighted in the rumours. It was the scandal of the Season!

Lord Templeton tried to trace the originator of the rumours, but no one seemed to know for sure. 'People had heard …' 'Someone had said …' The source could only be guessed at – supported by the disappearance of Signor Vitali from the London scene – and no parent was willing to add their own suspicions of that particular young man!

Nothing of which made Lucy's disgrace any less severe. Her mama's dire prediction had been correct. The eager young bucks faded away and invitations were no longer received and, as the Season drew towards its close without Lucy being even remotely likely to become betrothed in the near future, Lady Templeton withdrew her daughter from the glare of Society and the ignominy that surrounded her.

'Much of it is your own fault, Lucy!' she reminded her harshly. 'You had your chances and wilfully refused them all. Well, since you are determined to remain a maiden aunt, you had better learn what its consequences are likely to be. You will return to your sister at Glenbury Lodge until Society has found something else to gossip about. Then, and only then, might your papa see fit to recall you to Town! I am sure Marissa will find plenty for you to do, since their nurse has her hands full now that little Georgie has arrived. *You* shall take Bertie and Arabella off her hands and, since you need to learn the realities of life, you will go without your maid. That might teach you to appreciate what a privileged life you lead and your obligations to me and your papa!'

'Mama is very cross with you!' Marissa scolded her younger sister soon after receiving her into her drawing room. 'The wasted expense of it all. And think of those poor girls who had no offers made to them; they would give their eye-teeth to have been in your place.'

'Then they are likely to be glad to have the chance to set their cap at my rejected suitors themselves, now that I am removed from Town,' Lucy retorted. 'And they are welcome to them! Not a single one tugged at *my* heart-strings! I tell you, I have lost nothing by refusing them.'

'Nothing except the chance to be respectably married instead of becoming the talk of the Town! How *could* you, Lucy? Well, don't imagine your life will be a bed of roses here. Mama is determined that you will mend your ways and, hopefully, by next Season, Society will have forgotten your disgrace and *you* will be prepared to reconsider your actions – if any man is now rash enough to deem you a suitable wife.'

'*That* I shall never be!' Lucy declared with passion.

One of Lucy's first enquiries later that evening was about the health and well-being of Lady Montcliffe. 'For I would like to visit her when her period of mourning for the dowager is over,' she told her sister. 'She was very kind to me when I stayed with her last autumn.'

Marissa was startled. 'Oh! Did you not hear when you were in London? Both her sons were badly injured in the battle of Cuidad Rodrigo in January. As soon as Lady Montcliffe heard the dreadful news, she transferred herself and her household to Portsmouth to be near the military hospital where they were both fighting for their lives. For some reason, it was kept out of the newspapers, though I am not sure why. Someone must have pulled a few strings.'

'*Both* her sons?' Lucy echoed, remembering her brief encounter with the elder. She had suspected many times that it was the memory of the effects of his kiss that had made her so dissatisfied with the formal, clumsy love-making of the young bucks in London.

'Yes. Lord Rockhaven had rejoined his battalion just before Christmas and the two brothers fought alongside each other throughout the next few weeks. Lord Rockhaven was shot in the back whilst leaving the field of battle.' Marissa added with tight lips, 'Ugly rumours of cowardice and desertion bounced back and forth, though there has been no official confirmation of that.'

'Oh, surely not!'

Lucy's face paled. Whereas she hadn't been impressed by Lord Rockhaven's drunken behaviour, his embrace and kiss had made an indelible effect upon her. Her exciting time in London had dimmed the intensity of it, but she had no wish to hear such dire and shameful news. It contradicted all that she had previously heard about him. His grandmother would have been desolate had she lived to hear of it. And Lady Montcliffe – what must she be feeling?

'And they are both recovering?' she enquired, hopefully.

Marissa shook her head. 'Sadly, Conrad died in April. We have had no further news of the earl, but Montcliffe Hall remains shut up and there is no present expectation of it being reopened.'

'And it was Theo who was expected to die or be killed,' Lucy mused sadly, inadvertently using his given name, since that was how the dowager always referred to him. 'The Rockhaven curse has changed its course.'

'So it seems,' Marissa agreed sharply, 'but I don't want to hear any such nonsense talked about within the hearing of the children, or I shall regret agreeing to having you here again.'

Acting upon her mama's instructions, Marissa gave five-year-old Arabella into Lucy's sole charge, with seven-year-old Bertie being added in the afternoons after his return from the local rector's morning tuition.

Lucy's mornings were spent in the nursery schoolroom, teaching Arabella her numbers and letters, with very little interference from Nurse Harvey, who was more than happy to relinquish her care of the active girl into Miss Templeton's care and concentrate *her* lavish attention upon the new baby, whose demands were more basic and who thrived in the strict regime imposed upon him.

'I like having my lessons with you, Aunt Lucy,' Arabella confided after a few days in Lucy's care. 'You make everything so much fun.'

'And so it should be,' Lucy responded, giving her niece a hug. 'And, when Bertie is with us this afternoon, we are going out into the meadow to see how many different wild flowers we can find.'

'Can we take a picnic with us?'

'Of course! No outing can be considered worthy of its name if it doesn't include a picnic.'

Bertie wasn't impressed with the notion of collecting wild flowers, but was happier to hear that they would paddle in the stream afterwards and that he could take his favourite stable dog with them, called Wellington after the famous duke.

'I know where a big fat toad lives,' he generously shared with Lucy. 'Would you like to see it?'

'Certainly,' Lucy replied calmly, knowing he would rather she had screamed or fainted at the mere thought. 'I know where a few fat toads live near my home, as well.'

'Do you?' he admired, wide-eyed. 'I bet they're not as fat as *my* toad.'

'Probably not,' Lucy conceded kindly. 'Why don't you dig up a few fat worms to feed him with?'

'Shall I?' His face brightened. 'Right, I'll do that!'

And so, in mid-afternoon, the trio, dressed in their oldest clothes, set off through the kitchen garden and orchard into the meadow that lay beyond, accompanied by the excited young dog. The air was filled with the sweet fragrance of the mid-summer flowers that released their scent as they were brushed against. There were butter-cups, daisies, cornflowers and clovers, and many more all growing amidst knee-high grasses that waved in the light breeze. A small woodland bordered the meadow and Lucy hung the picnic basket from a low branch of a tree out of Wellington's reach.

'It will be safe there,' she informed her charges. 'Now, you know that you are not to go beyond the fence that borders your papa's land. Lord Rockhaven's gamekeeper won't want you running about on Montcliffe land frightening his pheasants.'

'I wouldn't frighten them,' Bertie informed her. 'I like birds. And, anyway, Lord Rockhaven's gamekeeper isn't there. Another man lives there now. I think he's a pirate. He sits in a chair on wheels and another man pushes him about sometimes, so he must be very old.'

Lucy raised an eyebrow at this impressive tale. 'What makes you think he's a pirate?'

''Cos he wears an eye-patch just like in my book!' Bertie said scathingly. 'And I bet he has a wooden leg too – only I've never seen it.'

'How do you know all this?' Lucy queried. 'Your mama hasn't said anything to me about it.'

Bertie shrugged. 'Nurse Harvey has been so busy with Georgie, she often lets us go out to play by ourselves, so I decided to do some exploring. I didn't take Bella, though. She'd be frightened of him.' He contorted his face as he added with relish, 'He looks very fierce and probably has a big cutlass to cut little girls into bits and pieces!'

Arabella stared at him wide-eyed. 'Don't tell such lies!'

she shouted, adding with bravado, 'But I'm not scared, so there!'

'Yes, you are, 'cos all girls are scared, aren't they, Aunt Lucy?'

'Not always,' Lucy countered. 'And I am not so sure you should be trespassing on Lord Rockhaven's land, especially if he has rented out his gamekeeper's cottage to someone else. But stop this squabbling, or else there'll be no paddling in the stream. Come on, let's see who can find the most flowers.'

With the incentive of competition, the two children were happily occupied for some time, plucking specimens from the ground and clutching them in their hot hands. When their interest waned, Lucy allowed them to splash in the nearby stream. They took off their shoes and stockings and scrambled down the sloping bank into the cool water and screamed with delight when Wellington joined them, barking and leaping and soaking the skirt of Lucy's frock as she sat on the bank with her bare feet dipped into the cool water.

'Take that dog somewhere else!' she commanded Bertie, jumping to her feet and shaking out her skirt. 'Let him chase rabbits or something, though I doubt he will catch any with his daft antics and all that noise. They'll be safe in their burrows before he even has scent of them.'

Bertie was happy to oblige, leaving Lucy and Arabella to enjoy the stream in a more sedate manner. It was only when Lucy became aware of the distant sound of dogs barking that she realized that Bertie had been absent for quite some time and deduced, quite accurately, that the cacophony of sounds was linked to her nephew and his dog.

'What is he up to, now?' she exclaimed. 'Come on, Arabella. We had better find him. Give me your stockings and just slip your feet into your shoes.'

Following the sound of the dogs, they hurried through the wood until they reached the fence that bordered their land. There was no sign of Wellington, but the frenzied barking continued ahead. With an exasperated sigh, Lucy lifted up her skirt and climbed the fence, giving a hand to Arabella. They hurried on. Lucy knew where they were going. She had played truant in these grounds herself when she had visited her sister in her younger days and had been bold enough to spy upon the gamekeeper at his work and peep through the windows of his small abode when he was busy elsewhere.

They came to a rough track that soon opened into a clearing. Here was the Montcliffe Hall gamekeeper's stone cottage. It had an air of neglect but was obviously being occupied as wisps of smoke were coming out of the chimney and drifting away amongst the trees. The dogs were barking around the back where, if Lucy remembered correctly, the previous gamekeeper had his kennels and a variety of outbuildings.

She hurried round the side of the dwelling to see Bertie trying to pull Wellington away from a large dish of some kind of meat which had been placed just within the open rear doorway of the cottage. Two other dogs were straining at their chains, howling their indignation at the evident theft that was taking place before them.

'Leave it, Wellington!' Bertie was shouting, pulling at his collar.

'Hey! What's going on?' a male voice shouted harshly.

From round the corner of one of the outbuildings came a man seated in a chair on wheels, just as Bertie had earlier mentioned. The man was propelling himself awkwardly along by the use of a pitchfork, its wooden handle pointing downwards. He was dressed in clothes similar to those of a gamekeeper, which might have supported his guise if Lucy hadn't known otherwise.

In spite of his disfigured face and the leather patch he wore over his left eye, Lucy knew that the 'old' man of Bertie's tale was none other than Theodore Lord Rockhaven, the Earl of Montcliffe!

Six

EVEN AS SHE recognized him, the man began to propel himself closer to the wide-eyed group but, to Lucy's dismay, the wheels of his roughly adapted chair hit the uneven edge of one of the cobblestones that formed the yard and the chair keeled over, tipping its occupant unceremoniously on to the hard ground.

'Oh, no!' Lucy gasped, picking up the hem of her skirt and running forward. The fallen man let out a thunderous oath and Arabella began to cry. Lucy turned back and drew the child close to her for an instant. 'Now, stop crying, Arabella. You are in no danger. He isn't angry at *you*. Bertie, attend to your sister and then get Wellington away from that bowl before he wolfs the lot!'

Letting go of Arabella, she ran to where Lord Rockhaven lay in an undignified sprawl and dropped down to crouch beside him. A spasm of pain crossed his face as he tried to raise himself up on his elbows.

'You are hurt, m'lord,' Lucy said needlessly. 'Can I help you to get up? Let me right your chair.' She rose to her feet and took hold of one of the handles of the fallen chair. 'Bertie, come and hold it steady whilst I help L—'

'Do … not … even … touch … me, woman!' Lord

Rockhaven snarled, each word enunciated separately, his lips drawn back in pain.

Lucy stepped back a pace, startled by his tone.

'But I must help you! I feel we were somewhat responsible for your fall.'

'Only *somewhat*? I would have said *totally*!' he snapped. 'And, yes, I am angry at you. You are trespassing, and allowing that mongrel to steal my dogs' food! Kindly take control of your charges and return to wherever it is you have come from.'

'Our offence was unintentional, so there is no need to be quite so churlish!' Lucy couldn't help snapping in return. 'Maybe if I can make you more comfortable, your temper will improve.'

'There is nothing wrong with my temper that your withdrawal will not put right. So, do as I say and be gone! And take this mongrel with you,' he said, pushing Wellington away from his attempts to lick his face.

Arabella burst into a fresh flow of tears and Lucy hovered uncertainly. In all honesty, she wished she could just leave him. It was what he deserved, the ungrateful man. But, how could she? He might be in a foul temper, but she supposed that was only to be expected, under the circumstances. Men didn't, as a rule, like to be seen to be at a disadvantage, did they? And this man was a mere shadow of his former self. 'I was only going to—'

'Damn you, woman! Do you not understand plain English? I do not wish for your help. Get those screaming children and your mangy dog off my property and leave me to get myself upright again.'

Unaccustomed to such harsh words, Lucy felt her cheeks

flushing, but her sense of compassion would not allow her to leave an injured man unattended in such circumstances, even if his current behaviour merited no kindness.

She gripped her lower lip between her teeth. 'I cannot do that,' she said firmly but quietly, 'but I know I cannot lift you either. Where is your…?' She hesitated to say 'servant' in case that was not the case. 'Is there not someone else living here with you? Another man? Where is he? He would be able to help to lift you.'

'You seem to know a lot about my living arrangements,' Lord Rockhaven snapped. His one visible eye narrowed with suspicion. 'Have you been spying on us? I sensed there was someone.'

'That … that was me, sir,' said Bertie, a little fearfully, hauling at the rope he had refastened to his dog's collar. 'And it wasn't me who was screaming. That was my sister. She can't help it, she's a girl.'

For a fleeting second, a glint of humour shone in Lord Rockhaven's eye but just as swiftly it was gone.

'You're trespassing,' he accused. 'Trespassers can be imprisoned … or even hanged!' He gritted his teeth against the pain in his hip. 'In the army, you'd be shot.'

Bertie looked crestfallen. 'Oh! I didn't know that. Wellington and I were playing at being scouts for the army and I saw you arrive in your cart. I'm trying to train Wellington to be a tracker dog. He seems to have a good nose for scenting things.'

'Huh! A good nose for food, no doubt,' Lord Rockhaven countered, wincing as another tremor of pain ran through him.

Bertie was oblivious to the sarcasm in Lord Rockhaven's

voice. He glanced back at the bowl of meat. 'Is it rabbit stew? It's Wellington's favourite, you know.' He looked intently at the man on the ground. 'Are you a pirate, sir? I think you must be, for you look fierce enough. What's the matter with your legs? Is one a wooden peg-leg?'

Lucy had listened in amazement to this exchange. It seemed Lord Rockhaven might have a spark of humanity in him after all, but the last personal question might well be a question too far! 'Quiet, Bertie! I don't think … oh, dear!'

Lord Rockhaven had sunk back on to the yard and his eye closed. She feared he had fainted. She dropped to his side again and laid her hand upon his forehead. Instantly, her wrist was grasped by his hand, causing her to jump. Startled, she looked down at him. It was disconcerting to look into his one eye but she tried to appear unconcerned. An unbidden memory of the touch of his lips upon hers swept across her mind and she felt her mouth go dry. Unconsciously, she parted her lips and ran the moist tip of her tongue over them. His face was too close for comfort and she tried to draw back, but his grip upon her wrist didn't allow her. Her cheeks flushed.

'Really, sir! I think perhaps you are not as injured as you appear!'

Lord Rockhaven ground his teeth. 'Do you, indeed? You think I would feign this undignified state? Have you no pity, woman?'

'None where it is not needed,' Lucy returned lightly, sensing that much of his anguish came from male pride. 'But I do wish you would let me try to help you regain your chair.'

He sighed heavily and sank back, releasing his hold on her. A shaft of pain low in his back made him close his eye again and he wondered why a faint vision of floating lemon silk seemed to dance in front of his closed lids. He opened his eye and refocused on the pretty face that hovered above him. He wondered who she was. She was too young to be the mother of the two children. Their sister, maybe? Or nursemaid? Did village children have nursemaids? He didn't know and the pain that racked his body took precedence over such idle musings. The girl's earnest concern caused him to speak more gently.

'Look, my man will be back soon. He will see to me. Go … and take your charges with you. You have ascertained that I am still alive, even if somewhat incapacitated. You may consider your duty done.'

'What if your man is delayed?' Lucy asked reasonably. 'Besides, if he is due back soon, then we may as well wait until he comes. Then at least we will know that you are once more in safe hands.'

'The Lord preserve me from meddling females,' Lord Rockhaven muttered, his tone not matching the piety of his words. 'Very well, since I am to get no peace until you are satisfied that you have fulfilled your role as the Good Samaritan, go into the cottage and get my greatcoat. It is hanging on a hook behind the door. And you, boy, push that dish of rabbit stew to where my dogs can reach it and maybe they will stop that infernal din!'

Disentangling Arabella's hold on her skirt, both Lucy and Bertie hastened to do as they were bidden, leaving Arabella standing nervously by herself, eyeing the fallen man warily, the tip of her thumb between her lips.

'I won't bite you, little miss,' Lord Rockhaven was saying, as Lucy returned with the heavy army great coat.

'Are you really a pirate?' Arabella asked, emboldened by Lucy's return.

'Huh!' Lord Rockhaven grunted. 'I might be. Would that frighten you?'

'No, though Bertie said it would. What's your name?'

'Mind your manners, Bella!' Lucy reproved her, aware that none of them had accorded to his lordship the courtesy due to a man of his rank and title, but intuitively sensing that he preferred to remain incognito for the time being. He obviously didn't remember *her*.

She leaned over him, beginning to lay the heavy coat over him. 'Here, let me tuck—' but her words were cut off by his answering Bella's question, 'My name's Rocky.'

Lucy paused, her glance drawn sharply to his face, faintly blushing at the speculative gleam his single eye portrayed. 'Isn't that a childish name for a grown man?' she snapped, attempting to cover her confusion.

Lord Rockhaven drew back his lips into what might have been intended as a grin but looked more like a wolf baring its teeth. 'As a children's nurse, you should be used to childish behaviour.'

'I'm not—' Lucy paused. So, he *didn't* recognize her. That wasn't surprising: he'd been too drunk to have been able to recognize his own face in a looking-glass! Well, if he wanted to play games of concealment, it was a game two could play. 'I am not accustomed to childishness from adults,' she amended her denial primly.

Lord Rockhaven shrugged as well as he was able in a prone position. 'How else should I behave when I am as helpless as a babe? Your two charges are more able than I.'

'You could try feeling less sorry for yourself!' Lucy retorted tartly, sensing that sympathy was the last thing he needed. 'What's happened has happened. Bemoaning the fact won't change it.'

'Easy to say.'

It was Lucy's turn to shrug. 'Yes. Your grandmother would have said to look upon it as a test of character.' Oh! She hadn't meant to say that!

His glance sharpened. 'You knew my grandmother?'

'Briefly.' Her voice was dismissive, but Lord Rockhaven persisted.

'Then you ...' – he glanced at Arabella, but she was now more interested in watching the dogs lapping up the rabbit stew – 'know who I am?'

Lucy didn't want to admit to their one meeting, just in case he *did* have faint memory of it. 'Your family resemblance is well known in these parts,' she said evading the personal question. Thankfully, it satisfied Lord Rockhaven.

'Exactly! Then you can understand why I do not wish it to be known that I am here.' His face twisted, though whether in actual or mental pain, Lucy wasn't sure. 'I have a great deal to work through. I cannot bear to do it under public gaze. I don't want *anyone* to know I am here. Do you understand?' He grasped her wrist again, his grip harder than he possibly realized.

Lucy winced but the intensity of his grip didn't lessen.

'Yes,' she acknowledged quietly. She did understand. Even the pity that was probably evident in her own eyes was more than likely obnoxious to him. 'I won't tell anyone, but the children might accidentally refer to meeting you.'

His eye held her gaze for a moment. Then he took a deep breath and sank back upon the cobblestones again, releasing his hold of her. Lucy immediately busied herself by tucking the ends of his coat under his body, twisting a sleeve into a pillow of sorts. Even in his injured state he exuded a feral power she knew little of, but she sensed a physical reaction surging through her body. She could readily believe that the rumours of his youthful exploits were based on fact. And didn't her own brief experience of him declare the same?

Lord Rockhaven twisted his head around to see the children watching the dogs devour their meal.

'Bertie, come here!'

Bertie turned at his name. 'Can I come and feed them again, sir?' he asked eagerly, as he ran over. 'I like dogs. I can help you train them and exercise them.'

'That's not a good idea at present, but I do need your help in another matter.'

'What sort of help?' Bertie demanded, intrigued by the request.

'Can you keep a secret?'

'Of course I can!' Bertie boasted. 'But I bet Bella can't. Girls are no good at secrets.'

'Yes, I can!' Arabella protested indignantly.

'What is the secret, sir?' Lucy asked, placing a restraining hand on Arabella's shoulder.

'It's very important that no one knows I am here,' he said simply, with disarming honesty.

'Gosh! Are you in hiding?' Bertie breathed eagerly. 'Are you really a pirate? Have you done something bad?'

Lord Rockhaven shook his head. 'I promise you I haven't done anything bad. I just want to stay here for a while until I get better. I don't want lots of *do-gooders* dropping in with their calves' foot jellies and sympathy.'

'Ugh!' Bertie agreed. 'I hate calves' foot jelly, too. We had to have it when we had chicken pox last year. We won't tell *anyone*, Rocky! Will we, Bella? Let's link little fingers and swear our promise.'

Lucy watched with amusement as Lord Rockhaven solemnly linked a finger with Bertie.

'And you, too, Aunt Lucy,' Bertie commanded. 'You can link with Bella and Rocky.'

Lucy wasn't sure it was wise to touch any part of Lord Rockhaven in such an intimate way, but it seemed churlish to refuse, so, with her cheeks blushing bright pink, she bent down and obligingly curled her little finger around the one Lord Rockhaven extended towards her.

He grinned wolfishly at her discomfort.

'So, *Aunt* Lucy? Will you keep my secret, too?'

'Of course … since that is what you wish,' she said a little stiffly.

The ceremony complete, she withdrew her finger from his grasp and straightened up, smoothing out the front of her skirt. She realized afresh that they were all dressed in old clothes. Lord Rockhaven probably thought they were local peasants from the village. Well, that suited her.

The sound of a horse's hoofs upon the cobbles drew their attention to the corner of the cottage and Lucy was relieved to see a dog-cart swing into the yard. The swarthy man on the driving seat was somewhat alarmed to see them and leaped down from his seat as Wellington strained at his leash to investigate the newcomer.

After an initial series of barks, Lord Rockhaven's dogs had calmed down and were now wagging their tails, which told Lucy that the man was Lord Rockhaven's companion. Bertie wasn't so easily appeased. He bravely jumped up and placed himself in front of Lord Rockhaven's prone figure, appointing himself as chief bodyguard, only relaxing seconds later. 'Oh, it's all right. It's your friend,' he announced over his shoulder, as the man hurried over, demanding, 'Now, now, what's happened 'ere?'

'He fell out of his chair,' Bertie informed him, 'and we can't lift him, but I 'spect you can.'

He was a large man, his body hard and muscular. He made as if to stoop over his master, ready to scoop him up into his arms, but Lord Rockhaven halted his progress with a one-eyed glare.

'My friend, Staines,' he introduced him somewhat abruptly. 'You may now leave me safely in his care.'

There was dismissal in his tone and Lucy knew that Lord Rockhaven did not wish them to witness the indignity of his helplessness as he was lifted back into his chair.

'I'm happy to meet you, Mr Staines,' she acknowledged the introduction. 'I'm sure we can leave ... Rocky ... in your care. Come along, children. It's time we went home.'

'Can we come to see you again?' Arabella, asked as she took hold of Lucy's hand.

'It's not advisable at the moment, little miss. It really is important that *no one* knows I am here. Remember your promise. We've sworn a solemn oath,' Lord Rockhaven reminded them. 'Now, leave me with my … friend.'

The children didn't argue and Lucy ushered them ahead of her, with Wellington reluctantly leaving the tempting aroma of the rabbit stew. When they reached the corner of the cottage, she couldn't help glancing back over her shoulder. Lord Rockhaven was seated in his chair with his coat draped over him. His face seemed drenched in pain and she marvelled that he had been able to conceal most of his discomfort in their presence. Maybe he had more strength of character than she had given him credit for. It would be interesting to find out.

In the meantime, she hoped his presence in the cottage remained a secret. Her sister wouldn't be overjoyed to hear they had visited an injured man in the gamekeeper's cottage even if she knew who he actually was.

Lucy grinned to herself. Maybe that should be *especially* if Marissa knew who he was, considering his past wild reputation.

Theodore Montcliffe, slumped uncomfortably in the wheelchair as Staines, his former batman, trundled him carefully into the dim interior of the humble cottage that was his present abode.

Drat the girl and her young charges. And that undisciplined dog. Wellington, indeed! His former commander was hardly honoured by the naming of the cur after him. He hoped the trio did indeed stand by their promise to keep his presence there a secret. His life might well depend on it.

'Arrgh!'

The cry had slipped involuntarily from his lips as the

chair jerked against the door jamb. Beads of sweat stood out on his forehead as he clenched his teeth together to suppress more grunts of pain. Hell! It hadn't hurt like this in all the time since the bullet had smashed into his back when he was carrying Con from the battlefield. Had his undignified tumble in the yard done some further damage? Drat the woman and those pesky children. The villagers had no business trespassing on his property. He'd have Staines put up some notices. 'Trespassers will be Prosecuted, Hanged, Drawn and Quartered!' *That* would keep out unwelcome intruders – *if* they could read, that is.

Back in the recesses of his mind, he knew he was being unfair, but the pain was excruciating.

'Sorry, Cap'n!' Staines apologized at once. 'Not quite got the hang of this contraption yet.'

Theo grunted a response. He hadn't got used to it either. He never would! He hated the thing. Yet it enabled him to get around to some extent. Anything was better than being entombed within the musty interior of the old cottage. However had Quilter put up with the cold dampness of the cottage for all those years? Huh, it was probably why he had had to be retired on a pension when his rheumatism made his life intolerable. He and Staines would be following suit if he were forced to live here much longer.

Why couldn't he just get up and walk, avenge his brother's death and get his life back to normal?

He had a restless night and awakened the next morning feeling as though a thousand fiery darts were being fired into him – into his back, his legs and his head. It was intolerable! He almost snatched the mug of amber liquid from Staines's hand and, by the time his former batman had assisted him in washing and dressing, he felt in control of the pain.

Unseasonal rain lashed against the cottage window, matching Theo's morose mood as he ate the food Staines brought to him. The man was no accomplished cook but he had learned how to put together whatever could be foraged from the Peninsular countryside and it kept body and soul together – just.

And body and soul needed to be brought together; that was why he was here, suffering this degradation, wasn't it? Determination was etched on his face as he wheeled himself across the cobbled yard and into a former pigsty in order to begin a series of self-imposed exercises, most of which, at the moment, involved the strengthening of the muscles in his arms and trying to establish some co-ordination between his one eye and a pistol in his right hand.

A few days ago Staines had constructed a pair of parallel bars set at the exact height to fit neatly under his former captain's armpits. Theo's first effort at traversing them had ended in ignominious defeat. His useless legs had defied his mental urging and the only progress forward had been when Staines had forced each leg to drag its way along the ground.

Theo now eyed the bars with a thunderous look that would have sent a shiver of fear through any human adversary.

'Set me on my feet, Staines!' he barked.

Staines did so. Theo waited until the wave of nausea caused by the action had passed away. Beads of sweat ran down his face as he mentally urged each leg in turn to move, but neither leg obeyed.

'Move, damn you!' he grunted to his legs. For a fleeting moment he felt as though the miracle had happened. He thought he felt the lower part of his body respond to his urging and take the weight from under his arms, but, the next instant, he sagged down again and no amount of urging brought the sensation back again.

'Come on, Cap'n,' Staines urged, forcing Theo's left leg forward. 'Put yer weight on that 'un. Now the other.'

With his help, Theo slowly worked his way along the bars but was then too exhausted to attempt to return in the same manner. He slumped his weight on the bars whilst Staines hurried to bring the wheelchair into position behind him. He had to face it, he was as helpless as a babe.

Seven

HEAVY RAIN FELL over the next two days and the afternoons were spent in the old nursery, now Arabella's schoolroom. Lucy hoped the children would forget about their friend Rocky.

Bertie knelt on the window-seat with his nose pressed up against the window as he watched the droplets chase each other down the pane.

'I can see two of each drops when my nose is pressed up against the window!' he announced with some satisfaction.

'That's because you are making yourself go cross-eyed,' Lucy reproved him patiently. 'Do come and play this game, Bertie. Your nose will be quite flattened if you keep it pressed up so ... and your eyes may stay crossed.'

'Like this?' Bertie asked, turning round, his eyes almost meeting at the point where his finger was pressing against the tip of his nose.

'Exactly like that.'

'You look like a pig.' Arabella declared.

Bertie gleefully snorted in response, not caring that it made the back of his throat and nose feel uncomfortable. 'I wish I was a pig. Then I could go out in the rain and get as dirty as I like.'

'You wish you *were* a pig,' Lucy corrected him carefully. 'But little pigs don't get raspberries and cream for tea and so, if I were you, I would change back into being a boy again. And, at the end of this game, I intend take any *nice* children down to the kitchen to see if Cook will let us bake some biscuits. However, if you don't wish to come...?'

She allowed her voice to trail away at the end of the sentence. Bertie immediately jumped down from the window-seat, his face brightening.

'Biscuits? Butter shortbreads? Or oaty ones with lots of sugar in them?'

'I'm sure Cook will let you choose.'

'Right!'

Thankfully, by the third day, the clouds were higher in the sky and markedly lighter in colour. Lucy scanned the sky hopefully.

'Yes, do take them out, Lucy,' Marissa instructed her. 'I couldn't rest yesterday afternoon with all the noise the children were making. It sounded as though they were charging up and down above my room like a herd of wild animals.'

Lucy suppressed a grin. That was *exactly* what the children had been playing at – Bertie was pretending to be Wellington chasing Arabella who, he said, was a frightened pony.

'But don't let them play in the stream,' Marissa continued. 'It will be flooding its banks after all that rain ... and *do* try not to bring the children home looking like two ragamuffins from the village. Nurse Harvey has many misgivings about letting you have a free hand with them. She says Bertie is becoming quite wild.'

'Nonsense! He is just being a boy. Anyway, we won't go to

the stream. We'll find other things to do. Maybe hide and seek in the wood? That should be fun.'

Marissa's 'humph' fell into empty space as Lucy had already made her escape and was on her way to tell the children to change into their old clothes as they were to go to play in the wood that afternoon. With a small feast of fruit and biscuits and bottles of Cook's homemade lemonade wrapped up in a small basket, they ran across the meadow and into the wood.

'I wish we could go and see Rocky,' Bertie declared. 'I think he must be quite lonely with only having his dogs and Staines for company.'

'No, Bertie. Lord ... I mean Rocky ... said quite firmly that he doesn't want any visitors just yet,' Lucy reminded him. 'We must respect his wishes.'

Bertie had a rebellious look on his face but he brightened up once the game of hide and seek began.

There followed a noisy half-hour of romping through the wood. Wellington, unfortunately, got the idea of the game very quickly and the only way they could continue was to tie him to a tree so that he didn't find the one who was hiding before his human companions. He barked his disapproval and was only released when neither Bertie nor Lucy could find Arabella and Lucy began to feel a little perturbed by her niece's absence.

Tail wagging, Wellington shot into the bushes with Lucy and Bertie close behind. Excited barking led them to Arabella's hiding place. She was crouched in the centre of a few straggling bushes adorned with a tangle of brambles.

'It was a good place, wasn't it?' she demanded, as she pushed Wellington's wet tongue away from her face.

'It was indeed,' Lucy agreed, ruefully inspecting her torn skirt.

Bertie glanced around with gleaming eyes. 'It's like a secret den, isn't it?' he declared. 'Can we eat our picnic in here?'

'A good idea,' Lucy agreed. 'Let's fetch the basket and we can have it right away.'

Bertie's imagination galloped ahead of him as they ate their picnic. 'We could make it even better with more branches, couldn't we? Then we can pretend we are pirates and hide our booty here.' He paused thoughtfully. 'We'll have to squeeze through the bushes carefully, then no one will ever find it!'

'That's a great idea,' Lucy commended him, glad that he had something other than Rocky to feed his imagination. 'There are lots of fallen branches for us to gather, but not today. We need to get some old gloves or our hands will be torn to shreds.'

The following afternoon, suitably protected by an odd assortment of gardeners' gloves, they made for the wood as soon as lunch was over and, over the next few days, they flung themselves energetically into finding suitable fallen branches and dragging them to the site of their den, with Wellington barking excitedly at their heels. Once the den was completed to Bertie's satisfaction, it became the base for their play activities. They played at hiding; being pirates; tracking each other through the wood; treasure hunting; collecting autumn fruits to later draw in the schoolroom, and ate their picnics sitting on a log they had dragged inside.

Although Lucy was happy that the children's thoughts

had been diverted from Lord Rockhaven to their new project, her own thoughts were intermittently drawn towards the wounded man and his self-imposed exile from Society. She felt she could understand his reluctance to be the object of people's pity and speculation, but how different his life now was from that of his youthful reckless exuberance. Not that his wildness had been attractive to her, but his freedom to be so was gone forever and she felt a vicarious sadness on his behalf.

Any pride Lucy felt at Bertie's self-discipline on the matter was dispelled when, a few days later, during a game of hide and seek, Bertie and Wellington disappeared. After spending some time searching for them, Lucy began to suspect that the disappearance was purposely contrived. Arabella's growing apprehension and guilty glances in the direction of the gamekeeper's cottage confirmed her suspicions.

'He said I wasn't to tell,' Arabella confessed when challenged. 'But he'll be all right, won't he? Rocky won't hurt him, even though he does look a bit frightening.'

'That isn't the point,' Lucy reproved her. 'Rocky doesn't want to risk anyone knowing where he is. Come on, we'd better go and see if we can catch up with Bertie before he gets there.'

That hope was dashed when they heard the dogs begin to bark and by the time Lucy hurried on to the scene, Bertie was standing on tiptoe looking in through the cottage window.

Lucy hurried forward and took hold of Bertie's arm.

'Come away at once, Bertie!' she remonstrated. 'You know very well Rocky doesn't want any visitors here. It's really quite naughty of you.'

'But I wanted to tell him about our den. He'll want to see it, I know he will!'

'Well, he can't. How would he get there, for one thing?'

'Staines would find a way,' Bertie confidently declared. 'But no one is here. I've looked in all the windows, but he wouldn't have left his dogs behind if he'd gone, would he? D'you think he's in one of the other buildings?'

'I don't know, Bertie, and, no, we aren't going to look. Now, do come away! And you, Wellington! That bowl is empty. I hope you haven't eaten the dogs' meal again.'

She hustled the boy and his dog away, followed by a now tearful Arabella holding on to her skirt.

Although there was no sign of either Lord Rockhaven or his companion, Lucy had the uncanny feeling that one or both of the two men were there but were choosing not to come into the open to be acknowledged. She couldn't blame them. Lord Rockhaven *had* made known his wishes to be left alone.

Over the next few days, Lucy's conscience smote her at times. It was all very well her having assumed that Lord Rockhaven and his man didn't want to be pestered by Bertie the other day, but what if they were in need of help? Could they be ill? The dogs' dish had been empty and she had no way of knowing just how long it had been so. Bertie assured her that Wellington had only licked around the edges.

'He wouldn't steal, you know,' he insisted.

'Dogs don't know if they are stealing or not,' she pointed out. 'All they know is the urge to eat any food that comes their way ... and Wellington is a prime example.'

She wished she might be able to make sure of the two men's well-being which would set her mind at rest. But she couldn't think how to manage it without taking the children with her. Her opportunity to make a visit on her own came unexpectedly when Marissa informed her that she was taking her two children to visit Arabella's godmother before she returned to London for the Little Season.

'We shall be gone for two or three weeks, Lucy, and, since Mama said I was not to take you into Society whilst you are with us, you must remain here. I trust you will be mindful of our good standing in the community and amuse yourself with ladylike pursuits. Without the responsibility of looking after Bertie and Arabella you will be able to practise your music and sewing. Indeed, I shall expect the tapestry you brought with you to be finished on our return. Oh, and I have instructed Cook to make up some food parcels for you to distribute to the poor in the village. It is time you became more aware that not everyone is as fortunate as ourselves. I am sure it will make you more appreciative of the obligations placed upon us by our position in Society. Use the gig whenever you wish. One of the outdoor staff will accompany you, if you give enough warning to Campden to arrange it.'

Lucy murmured a noncommittal response, her initial disappointment at being left behind on her own apart from the servants being overtaken by the realization that she would be beholden to no one during her sister's absence. Thank goodness Marissa's compliant character and her lack of imagination rendered her unable to envisage Lucy's joy at such unprecedented freedom! Not that she would behave in any fashion that might bring disgrace upon her sister's family. That would be foolish indeed and would bring their mama's wrath upon her head. But to be able to go out without endless questions both before and afterwards was a delight too attractive to be missed.

Consequently, a few days later, no sooner had the family coach, followed by a more modest conveyance containing their trunks, Rupert's valet, Marissa's personal maid and Nurse Harvey, trundled in procession down the drive, than Lucy put on a serviceable walking dress, collected a loaded basket from Cook – and Wellington from his stable kennel – and set off briskly through the wood to the gamekeeper's cottage, hoping that no one would notice that her objective was in the opposite direction from the village. Without the distractions caused by the children's presence, she was there in less than fifteen minutes.

Allowing Wellington to respond briefly to the indignant welcome by the chained dogs, she bade him, 'Quiet, Wellington! Come to heel', and knocked boldly on the door.

When there was no response she faced the cobbled yard with its assorted outbuildings, the backs of her hands upon her slender hips. Where were they? All she wanted was to know they were all right. Should she investigate further?

A sound behind her made her turn back towards the door. It was now pulled open and Lord Rockhaven was manoeuvring his wheelchair into the opening.

'Oh!'

His face was less than welcoming and, even though he was seated in his wheelchair, he exuded a feral presence. For a moment Lucy was rendered speechless and she simply stared at him, aware that a warm flush was rising over her face. She now felt guilty at being found upon his doorstep. She shouldn't have come; he had made it clear he didn't want company.

'Well?' Lord Rockhaven demanded. 'I presume you are here for a purpose? Or were you just passing by?' He peered past her. 'And where are your young charges? You haven't left them alone in the wood, have you?'

His challenging tone roused Lucy from her confusion. 'Good day, Lord Rockhaven. A little civility wouldn't go amiss. I can tell you haven't had much practice at receiving visitors … or perhaps you have frightened them away by your abrupt manner. And, no, I haven't left the children in the wood. They are … away … at the moment. Get down, Wellington! Lord Rockhaven doesn't want his face licked!'

Wellington immediately sat down, his tongue hanging from his open mouth as he surveyed the confrontation.

'At least *he* does as he's told,' Lord Rockhaven growled. 'I always knew dogs had more sense than people.'

'And at least *I* have a social conscience!' Lucy retorted in retaliation. 'I was worried about you. When there was no sign of you last week when we called—'

'In flagrant defiance of my request that you stay away,' Lord Rockhaven was swift to interject.

'Yes … well, it was quite unintentional on *my* part!' Lucy hastened to assure him sharply, lest he think she felt any sort of feminine tenderness towards him. 'It was … well, Bertie felt concerned about you and slipped away without my knowledge.' She could hardly bear to look at his face, so thunderous was his expression. However, not one to give up

at the first hint of discouragement, she hurtled on, 'And ...
er ... afterwards, I ... I feared you might have been ...
harmed ... in some way. So, I came on my own today to
make sure you are well ... and to ... er ...' She glanced down
at the basket that hung on her arm.

'To bring me some morsel of food, I suppose. Well, I don't
need charity!' Lord Rockhaven snapped. 'If I had a need of
anything, I would send Staines to buy it ... and I told you not
to tell anyone I am here! I suppose your employer is now
busybodying about the village, telling everybody she meets.
Good God, woman! I know I made it seem like a game to the
children but it's no game, believe you me. My very life might
be now in danger thanks to you and your meddling!'

His hands dropped to the large wheels at the side of his
chair and, with a snort of fury, he began to reverse into the
cottage.

'I have told no one!' Lucy snapped back. 'Neither have the
children. Speaking of whom, they have better manners than
you and would be showing some gratitude for a neighbourly
visit!'

Her words halted him. 'Ha! A neighbourly visit, is it?
Trespassing more like! Don't think I don't know you bring
those children to play in my wood every day, vandalizing my
trees.'

'It isn't *your* wood and we have done no vandalizing. We
were building a pirates' den there. Oh!' Her free hand flew
to cover her mouth. 'I'm sorry! I didn't mean ...' She paused,
suddenly aware that he was probably self-conscious of his
disfigurement and might take offence at the children's
assumption that he was a pirate, even though he had gone
along with the idea the day they met.

A look of exasperation swept across Lord Rockhaven's face and he slumped back into his chair. When he spoke, it was in a more conciliatory tone. He waved a hand towards her vaguely.

'Your words do not hurt me. I'm sorry … it is I who should be apologizing. You are right: my behaviour is appalling. It's just that it's true I am playing no game. I have enemies and, as you see, I am at somewhat of a disadvantage if they track me down.'

In spite of the bitterness of the last few words, Lucy was aware of stirrings deep within her; stirrings she didn't fully understand because those parts of her body were never mentioned, but they were part of her and she wondered why this bantering conversation should affect her body in a similar way to when she had been briefly held in his arms a year earlier. It certainly wasn't physical attraction. His scarred face was pale and thin and his one visible eye glared at her with reproof.

Yet, she knew he hadn't ceased to invade her thoughts since their recent encounter and, in her mind's eye, he was brutishly handsome and still had the power to melt her insides to a molten heat. She felt the impulse to reach out and touch his cheek and smooth away the vivid scar, and run her fingers through his dark hair, which, seated as he was in the wheelchair, was tantalizingly close!

Alarmed by the intensity of her longings, she thrust her free hand behind her and stepped back.

Lord Rockhaven's eyebrow rose fractionally at her sudden movement. 'I won't bite you,' he said drily, as if he could read her thoughts and was amused by them.

Her cheeks flushed. 'I didn't suppose you would,' she said

primly. 'I just … didn't want to crowd you.' Good heavens, even in a wheelchair this man affected her more than any of the handsome bucks and dandies in London.

No, all she felt for him was pity for his unfortunate vulnerable state. She just wanted to help him to sort himself out – to, quite literally, help him to get back on his feet. Wouldn't anyone who had known the vigorous young man of former years feel that same? Except she knew she was lying to herself; she wanted him back on his feet so that he could hold her in his arms again and kiss the life out of her.

With a start, she realized Lord Rockhaven was speaking and pushed her errant thoughts away, though she knew she would savour them later.

'And you have told no one, you say? No one else knows I am here?'

Lucy shook her head. 'No. Your secret is safe. I don't understand, though. You are a lord … an earl, even. You must have influence. If you have enemies, cannot you bring a charge against them? Cannot the authorities act on your behalf? Why do you have to go into hiding? You said you have done nothing wrong, or was that just to appease the children?'

'No. I spoke the truth: I have done nothing wrong, but I have no proof of what my … enemy … has done against me. I just know he will not leave it at this.' He indicated his person and Lucy assumed he meant his disability. 'He will try again and I don't intend to make it easy for him, but I need time.'

'Time for what?' Lucy asked.

'To get better, of course! I won't be shot in the back again. Next time, he will have to face me man to man.'

Lucy stared at him. 'Someone tried to kill you *deliberately*? I thought you had been wounded in battle – at least, that is what everyone says – that you were both injured and that your brother ... died.'

Her voice faltered as she recollected what else Marissa had said. She felt embarrassed that her sister should have repeated slanderous gossip and her discomfort was made worse when Lord Rockhaven himself spoke aloud her inner reflection.

'Huh! And no doubt these know-alls embellished the truth with innuendoes of us leaving the battle whilst it was still in progress, labelling us as deserters!'

Lucy touched his arm in compassion for his distress. 'People will always relish a touch of scandal. It is best to ignore their gossip and get on with life. It must have been a dreadful time for you, especially since you are ...' Again, her voice faltered to a standstill. What was it about this man that made her senses fly off in all directions?

'A cripple? Don't let your fine feelings stop you from saying the word, Miss—' He broke off, as if not knowing her name was a further indication of his crippled state. His shoulders sagged momentarily, then he banged the heel of his right hand against the armrest of his wheelchair. 'It should have been *me* who was killed! Con saw him take aim and leaped to push me aside, taking the bullet meant for *me*. He spoke his name as I stooped to lift him over my shoulder. The next bullet passed through him and got me also. I lived ... but Con didn't. I failed him. It should have been me! It was *my* lot in life to die young, not *his*!'

'Huh! Because of the so-called *curse*?' Lucy exclaimed, sensing that a soothing reply would inflame his morose state. 'How ridiculous! You are an intelligent man, how can you believe such nonsense?'

Lord Rockhaven's face flushed at her tone. 'What do *you* know about it? My ancestors have died by the *nonsense*! I always knew how it would end, but not the manner of it. But it should have been me. Not Con. *I* am the elder son.'

'Stop feeling sorry for yourself,' Lucy retorted, realizing that he felt guilty to have survived whilst his brother had not. 'Would Conrad have felt any better if he were the survivor? I suspect not. You have lost a dearly beloved brother, but it was not your fault! Stop blaming yourself and get on with living. I am sure that is what your brother would have wanted you to do.'

'You call *this* living?' Lord Rockhaven demanded angrily, banging both his fists down on the arms of his wheelchair. 'It is worse than death, I can tell you!'

Lucy could think of nothing to say that would not sound condescending or patronizing and, after a pause, Lord Rockhaven spoke in a more even tone. 'Now, if you don't mind, gossiping over my threshold will get me nowhere. I have things to do.' He waved a deprecatory hand towards her basket. 'Take your offerings to more deserving cases.'

It was a clear dismissal and although it hurt her pride to turn away and retrace her steps through the wood, she did so with as much poise as she could muster. He didn't even wait until she was out of sight before he returned indoors. She heard the fall of the latch when she was no more that six paces from his door.

He was insufferable and deserved to be abandoned to his fate!

Eight

THEO'S CHIN SANK on to his chest within the dim cottage. That was all he needed: well-meaning females with nothing better to do than to be on his doorstep with delicacies to tempt his appetite. His eyes narrowed as he speculated on their two confrontations. She knew who *he* was, but who was *she*? She certainly wasn't anyone he had met socially ... he would have remembered her. She was pretty and vivacious and would have caused a quickening of his blood if he had met her before his incapacitating injury. Not that anything serious could have come of it, of course, but he was sure he could have come to a suitable arrangement with her. Her lips looked decidedly kissable and she had a degree of spirit. He grinned as he recalled her lively banter, then swiftly sobered. She had *too much* spirit, he corrected himself, recalling her outspoken reproof of him.

What did *she* know of suffering? Nothing! It was obvious that she had never experienced any severe disappointments in life. A bit of suffering would do her good, he decided morosely.

Was that why he had taken some perverse pleasure in knocking back her well-meaning act of kindness towards him? A little unchivalrous of him perhaps, but it had certainly wiped the condescending smile from her face.

He slapped his hand against the armrest of his chair and grimaced in self-disgust. He knew he wasn't being fair to her. She hadn't been condescending at all, but he had felt himself at a severe disadvantage. Wouldn't any man without the use of his legs feel thus if a pretty young woman came calling on him? What else other than pity could any female feel towards him in his present state? And he didn't want pity from *anyone*, let alone an attractive girl who gave him longings he had thought himself incapable of experiencing again!

A vision of her face flashed before him. Ringlets of deep russet caught up on her head, with a few wayward curls falling beside her cheeks ... cheeks that were a shade too rosy by social standards of the day, no doubt due to her freedom of the outdoors. No, she wasn't anyone from his own level in society, he was sure of that.

Yet, somewhere in the back of his mind, he felt he ought to know her. Felt he *did* know her! A fleeting wisp of an elusive image once again hovered on the fringe of his memory, but it melted away like the early morning mist evaporates in the heat of the sun. Ponder as much as he might, he couldn't remember having met her until that unfortunate spillage from his chair.

Perversely, he couldn't let it go. Was she the parson's daughter? Her demeanour, her voice and choice of language spoke of a genteel education. But no, the parson's daughters were older – unless a new parson had been appointed in his absence – and if that were the case, he hadn't met his daughters. Maybe she was a village girl who had been in employment at Montcliffe Hall? His mother would have given encouragement to any servant who showed signs of promise and might have taken her under her wing. That would explain her knowledge of his family and of the curse that hung over them.

A fresh surge of indignation flowed over him. How dare she belittle it so! It had dominated his life for as long as he could remember. Only his grandmother had spoken of it dismissively, blaming, instead, the excesses of his ancestors on his father's side of the family. Had they felt as he did? That if they were to die young they might as well enjoy life to the full whilst they could?

Well, there was no enjoyment in life now, was there?

A renewed frenzy of barking from the dogs and the rumble of cartwheels on the cobbled yard dragged him out of his reverie. Good. Staines was back with more stores. It was time for his daily exercise. In anticipation, he slowly lifted each foot in turn, flexed his ankle and then lifted and straightened each leg. It took some effort and concentration but at least he was making some progress now. All he needed was more time.

Lucy's mind was also engrossed in thinking about the confrontation. Much as she determined to forget about him, she couldn't help being intrigued by the man and his predicament, but he had made it very clear that he didn't want any sort of help or sympathy from her or anybody else. For all she knew, he might be romanticizing what had happened to him and his brother on the battlefield. Why would someone from his own ranks shoot at him and Conrad? Someone whom they knew by name? If it were true, why hadn't he denounced the person?

She sighed sadly. Maybe it was simply that he was unable to face the reality of what had happened? That he had been so terrified by the horrors of frenzied slaughter that surrounded him that he and his brother had made an attempt to flee the scene of battle and had been shot as deserters by a superior officer? And what sane and rational person could hold him and his brother in condemnation? Who knew how they or anyone else would behave in the horrific trauma of the battlefield?

Yet, somehow, that thought didn't rest easily upon her. Theodore Rockhaven, Earl of Montcliffe was made of sterner stuff than that. He was no coward. He would face adversity head-on even if he was physically unfit to do so.

And that worried her.

Life without the constraints of her sister and her family did not entirely live up to the life of freedom that Lucy had imagined. To her chagrin, she discovered that even the servants had certain expectations of her behaviour and every step outside those expectations drew censorious raising of eyebrows and even mild reproofs from the older ones – her solitary outing in the wood being the first of many such condemned activities. Not that Lucy intended to repeat *that* exercise, so Cook's admonition was an unnecessary rebuke.

She tried to convince herself that she was indifferent to the young earl, whatever his predicament, but, deep in her heart, she knew that wasn't true and she couldn't stop thinking about him, acknowledging a reluctant admiration for his determination to restore his fitness, even if his driving reason for doing so might hinge on a misapprehension of what had actually happened on the battlefield. She also had to acknowledge that something deep within her stirred with longing in spite of her declared intention never to trust a man again. It puzzled her. Why, despite his abrupt rudeness towards her, did she long to further their acquaintance?

Determined to push her thoughts of Lord Rockhaven out of her mind, Lucy flung herself into other activities to fill her days. In the mornings, she rode around the nearby countryside accompanied by a groom determinedly keeping away from Montcliffe land, and in the afternoons, when the sun was at its hottest, she followed more leisurely pursuits, played her favourite pieces on the piano, did some stitch work or arranged flowers she had picked from the garden.

Those genteel activities palled after a few days and, desperate for something more to do, she volunteered to take some food parcels to the local villagers. Cook readily agreed as she had plenty of other tasks for her kitchen staff in the absence of the family; tasks that could only be done in their absence, such as thoroughly cleaning the upstairs rooms and sorting out the store cupboards.

So, at ten to two in the afternoon, the gig was harnessed to an amiable pony named Maud and brought around to the front of the house by a red-faced stable lad, who willingly handed over the reins to the charming sister of his mistress when she declared that she would drive the gig herself.

'I will be quite safe in the village by myself, Higgins,' she confidently assured him when he made to climb up on the rear step, 'and I am sure there is plenty of other work for you to be doing.'

Higgins tipped his cap and returned to the stable yard,

unsure if he were happy to be relieved of the duty, or disappointed to have been refused the opportunity of an outing.

Lucy smiled happily as she flicked the reins, relishing in the freedom of being unaccompanied. She was determined to make the most of it in Marissa's absence. Maud happily trotted along the country lanes to the nearby village and could probably have done so without Lucy's hand upon the reins. She could be goaded into a smarter pace by a gentle flick of the whip above her head and snorted her appreciation of the reward of an apple when they arrived at the village, where Lucy tethered the pony by the village green.

As she walked from cottage to cottage, she smiled and bade, 'Good afternoon,' to anyone she met and, the next time she went, made sure she had a bag of Cook's homemade confectioneries to dole out to the children she encountered playing around the green or in their homes.

Lucy's unaffected friendliness quickly changed any initial distrust from the villagers into a mutual cordiality. Her pleasure as she delved into her basket and her exclamations of delight over Cook's selections melted away any resentment they might have felt and before the week was over she was warmly welcomed into the humble cottages.

It amazed her that whole families could live in such small dwellings. Why, there was hardly more than a single room that served as kitchen, dining room and an extension to the sleeping area that was partitioned off by a piece of old sailcloth – if the bundle of what seemed to be bedding in the corner was indeed what she supposed it to be. Where did they wash or have any degree of privacy?

The cottages varied in degree of cleanliness and in what passed as furniture. Clothes and possessions were minimal and Lucy was astute enough to realize that their simple lifestyle was, in reality, a struggle to survive. She was glad that her sister had a social conscience and that she tried to help them. So would *she*, if she were ever in a position to do so, she resolved.

'You'm a real treasure, my dear,' one mother declared a few days later, when a chicken pie was placed upon her table followed by a bread and butter pudding.

Lucy popped a piece of butter fudge into the mouths of the four young children who clung wide-eyed to their mother's skirt.

'It's a pleasure, Mrs Boulton,' she murmured, smiling at the children as traces of fudge oozed from the corners of their mouths.

'It do help my Georgie keep body and soul together, especially since the 'all was closed down,' the woman continued. 'Eh, I knows the family has had its tragedies but we do miss her ladyship. We 'as our 'opes that she may come back some day. No one seems to know what has become of his lordship – that's what I told the gentleman only this morning. No, I sez, and if her ladyship herself don't know where he is, then how can you expect the likes of us to know?'

Lucy's heart immediately leaped in alarm. 'Someone was here, asking about Lord Rockhaven?' she asked sharply. Her heart was beating faster as she spoke his name. 'Did he say who he was?'

'Eeh, no, miss. He had no needs to declare himself to the likes o' me. A bit high an' mighty, he was, too. I was glad not to be able to help him.'

'What did he look like? Was he young? Or old?'

A surge of excitement leaped within her as she realized

that she now had a genuine reason for contacting Lord Rockhaven again and that she might be of some use to him.

'Well, he weren't old, miss – that is, he was older than you, but not as old as me.' She screwed up her face as she sought to recollect the man's features. 'He was dark-haired and dark-skinned, like a lot o' these wounded soldiers we see traipsing the country. And his man looked much the same.'

'His man? He wasn't on his own, then?'

'Eeh, no, miss. No one of 'is class trying to impress would travel on his own. But he didn't impress me none. Dressed fit to kill, he was. A right clown! And him with as rough-looking a fellow as I've ever seen. I wouldn't like to meet 'im on a dark night on me own.' She shuddered and clasped her hands over her ample bosom, before continuing in a confidential manner, 'Thinking of the upper-class one, I suppose I shouldn't say this, but he had a look of the late earl. The same long nose, though nowhere near as handsome, and he looked at *me* as if I were something he'd trodden in. That weren't like the late earl at all. He was a real gentleman, he was … though a wild and reckless one. His sons took after him, God bless their souls, if his young lordship's dead, that is. D'you think you might know him, miss?'

'No, no, I just wondered, that's all.'

But she felt the man seemed to fit in with Lord Rockhaven's fears that someone who had been fighting on the Peninsular might have a motive in tracking him down. He could be genuine, of course. Someone making enquiries on behalf of Lady Montcliffe. Maybe even a relative, if Mrs Boulton's recognition of a family resemblance were correct. But, surely, he would have declared his name if that were the case. No, his questioning was being done in a secretive way and it was best to take no chances. After all, Mrs Boulton hadn't taken to him, had she?

So she enquired, 'Is he still in these parts, do you know?'

Mrs Boulton nodded her head. 'It's said he's staying at the Eagle and Child and that he'll pay well for any information, but he won't get nowhere with his questions round hereabouts. Besides, no one has seen his lordship since he was here a year or so ago. They do say, though, that *someone* is living in old Quilter's cottage – that's the old gamekeeper, miss. I doubt you'd remember him. Been gone a few years, he 'as. The lads 'ave seen signs of someone there – not his lordship, o' course – someone more like an ex-soldier who's been pensioned off, but I don't know the truth o' that. Eeh, the lads won't get into trouble for being on his lordship's land, will they? They don't mean no 'arm; they just catch the odd rabbit or suchlike to fill their families' bellies.'

'No, of course not,' Lucy hastened to assure her, hoping she spoke the truth. 'Er, the man who was making enquiries, did you tell him about the ex-soldier living in Quilter's cottage?' she asked anxiously.

'Eh, no, miss. He got no more out o' me than he deserved, and that was nowt! But I can't speak for everyone else, o' course. Especially once they have some ale in them.'

That was true, Lucy reflected. And even a hint about a man's presence in the cottage could mean discovery of Lord Rockhaven and Staines, if Lord Rockhaven's fears were founded on fact and not fantasy. So, she needed to return there as soon as possible to warn him and brave his possible wrath once more. She grinned to herself at the thought of his reaction to another visit from her. She felt no alarm at that thought: she would give as good as she got.

She speedily delivered the remaining groceries to Cook's designated recipients and, no more than ten minutes later, she was on her way towards the Montcliffe estate. She had been careful not to make her departure from the village seem hurried in any way and only flicked the whip over Maud's head when she had driven past the last humble dwelling. She would have preferred to approach the cottage on foot through the wood, since that was less noticeable, but she didn't dare waste the time.

Desperately hoping that she was in time to warn Lord Rockhaven of the possible danger he was in, she turned off the country lane on to the track that led to the game-keeper's cottage. She didn't want to herald her approach in case the man making enquiries were already there, so she turned off the track before she reached the cottage and drove a few yards into the woodland, thankful that the weather had been dry recently, leaving the ground reason-ably firm. She tethered Maud to a low bush and then hurried towards the cottage.

She paused behind a tree and peered round it, glad that she was wearing a dark-green carriage gown so that she blended in with the woodland. There was no sign of any visi-tors. She listened. All seemed quiet. The dogs had begun to bark, but not in a frenzied way, which was a good sign. They had detected her presence but couldn't do anything other than warn of her approach. She must point that out – it could alert an enemy that there was someone who needed the dogs' protection. She flitted to the next tree and then the next and then ran lightly across the open space to the cobbled yard.

Staines was standing by the old outbuilding watching her approach.

'Afternoon, miss. We thought as it might be you, seeing as how the dogs weren't too anxious. T'cap'n sez as he hopes you don't mind but he's too busy to converse with 'ee right now.'

Lucy laughed out loud. 'I bet he said it a lot more colourfully than that!' Her eyes twinkled merrily for a moment but then swiftly sobered. 'It's vitally important that I see him. Is he in there?'

Staines didn't stand aside. 'He don't want to be disturbed, miss.'

'I'm sorry, but I must. It's important. There have been enquiries made about him in the village.'

Something in her quiet determination told Staines that this wasn't just an annoying social call. 'All right, miss. If you'll wait here ...'

He turned and pushed open the door, intending to go inside first to speak to his master, but Lucy moved swiftly in his wake and entered the dim, low-ceilinged building only one pace behind him.

'It's the young lady, Cap'n. She says—'

'It's all right. I'll tell him myself,' Lucy said behind him. She stopped and gaped at the earl. 'You're standing!' she exclaimed. 'Can you walk? Are you getting better?'

Lord Rockhaven was indeed standing between two sets of parallel bars, his arms over the top bars and his hands gripping two lower ones. His face darkened and then flushed.

'I would have appreciated—'

Lucy took a step forward, pushing aside the surprise of finding Lord Rockhaven on his feet. 'I'm sorry. I didn't intend to rush in unannounced, but there isn't time for any social niceties. Two men have been asking about you in the village. A gentleman and his servant. I came to warn you. I don't think anyone knows that you are here and, from what I gather, they would be unlikely to give you away, even if they did, but they seem to know that Mr Staines is here – except they don't know who he is – only that he is likely to be an ex-soldier taking shelter.'

She paused for breath, giving Lord Rockhaven the chance to ask sharply, 'Who is he? What does he look like?'

'I haven't seen him, but one of the villagers said he is about your age and has a slight family resemblance.' She raised her eyebrows questioningly as she said the latter phrase, noticing that Lord Rockhaven didn't seem surprised by the revelation. 'The man with him seems a bit of a rough-neck and best avoided.'

'When did he arrive?' Lord Rockhaven asked, breaking eye contact to demand, 'My chair, Staines.'

Staines hurried to wheel it into the appropriate position, murmuring, 'Sorry, Cap'n. I didn't think anyone had seen me.'

Lucy replied to Lord Rockhaven's question, 'Only today. Mrs Boulton didn't think anyone would deliberately betray you, but feared someone might mention Mr Staines without thinking. It's some village lads who have noticed you here, Mr Staines.' She turned back to Lord Rockhaven, a note of reproof in her voice as she added, 'The villagers are quite poor, you know, especially since the Hall was closed down. Many are out of work and have to catch rabbits and such-like to be able to feed their families. And I really think you should let your dogs roam loose for the time being and maybe find somewhere else to live for a while. Isn't there anywhere up at the Hall? It would be more suitable.'

Lord Rockhaven's face was grim and he didn't acknowledge her suggestions. He was too busy manoeuvring his chair deftly towards the doorway.

Staines leaped out of his way. 'T'lass is right, Cap'n. We needs to get you away from here without delay. You're a sitting target in that chair.'

Theo grimaced at Staines's words. Didn't he know that! 'I'm not running away,' he snapped. 'If my cousin has the temerity to come here to kill me, he'll find me ready and waiting for him! He won't shoot me in the back as he did last time!'

'Your cousin?' Lucy echoed, horrified that a family member should be the one who had tried to kill Lord Rockhaven and, presumably, *had* killed his brother.

'He is a braggart and a wastrel and, since Con's death, he, unfortunately, is my heir,' Lord Rockhaven said tersely. 'His extravagances have brought him to *point non plus* and he has his greedy eyes on my title and fortune. I refuse to run away from such a character.'

'Nay, it's not running away,' Staines argued. 'It's a tactical manoeuvre … just until you're stronger, Cap'n. Let him find *me*. I'm only what folks think, an ex-soldier tekin' shelter. I'll humbly apologize and move on me way until he's gone.'

Theo could see the sense in that. If they both suddenly disappeared, it would look too providential to be a coincidence. 'What if he recognizes you? His companion sounds like that thug of a batman he had.'

'I'll tell him 'er ladyship says as 'ow I could come here. From what you've said about 'er, she would 'ave if she knew.'

'That might satisfy him…. However, I won't get far in this,' he pointed out, still reluctant to protect himself and leave his servant behind.

'What about the children's den?' Lucy suggested. 'It's incredibly well-hidden though it offers no protection against the weather.' She looked at him doubtfully. 'You might have to stay there overnight.'

Theo looked at Staines. 'Would it do?'

'Aye, I reckon it would. They've made a good job of it and I put some added branches there to make it thicker.' He looked apologetically at Lucy. 'I 'ope you don't mind, miss. It reminded me of when I was a lad.'

Theo made a swift decision. 'Right! We need to move fast then. I'll need a couple of those old horse blankets out of the stable, Staines, and my greatcoat from the cottage. Oh, and a cob of bread and my canteen of water … and anything else that might betray my presence here.'

Staines hurried across the yard towards the cottage.

'I'll get the blankets. Is that the stable over there?' Lucy asked, pointing to her right.

'Yes. They're hanging on hooks near the door. Two should be enough.'

Lucy darted across the yard. Staines was emerging from the cottage when she returned clutching the blankets. They smelled of horses, but she didn't suppose a seasoned campaigner like Lord Rockhaven would find the smell offensive, nor the texture too rough.

Staines dropped a bundle on his master's lap and then draped the blankets on top.

'I'll take Bruno with me,' Theo decided. 'He's a good watch dog and will keep quiet on command.'

The two dogs had been whining and grumbling during the recent activity and their noise increased at the prospect of imminent release.

'Quiet!' Staines commanded, as he entered the pen, separating Bruno from the other dog. Bruno, tail wagging, willingly squeezed through the gate that Staines held only partly open and bounded over to where Lucy stood beside Theo. She felt only a vague unease, realizing that neither man would have released the dog if it was likely to harm her. She stood still whilst the dog sniffed around her.

'Friend!' Theo said quietly. Bruno immediately transferred his attention to his master, who heartily scratched the dog's ears. 'Good boy!' Theo praised, and then said more sharply, 'Patrol!'

Bruno stood still, only the muscles along his back and haunches quivering as he tensed for action.

'Don't forget to dismantle all my training equipment and scatter it in the outbuildings as soon as you come back, Staines,' Theo remembered to say.

'I'll do that, Cap'n. Now, 'old on tight. We're off.' Staines took hold of the wheelchair handles and set off at a trot, trundling the wheelchair over the cobbled yard and along the track towards the wood.

Bruno loped alongside and Lucy hurried to keep up.

Once they left the hardened track she could see that the wheels were leaving two narrow parallel ruts along the ground. Careless of her smooth hands, she grabbed hold of a fallen branch and began to sweep vigorously across the tell-tale evidence.

They reached softer ground and the wheels sank too far into the ground to allow Staines to make much headway.

'It's not much further,' he told his master. 'If it's all right with thee, Cap'n, I'll carry thee. Can you fetch t'rest o' things, miss?'

Lucy gathered them up from Lord Rockhaven's lap and turned away, sensitively realizing that Lord Rockhaven would not wish her to watch as Staines gathered his tall yet slender form into his arms and expertly draped him over his shoulder. Staines set off in the direction of the den, loping along as if he had no more than a sack of grain over his shoulder. Lucy dropped the assorted bundle on to the seat of the wheelchair and yanked the wheelchair around, knowing it would be easier to pull it through the long grasses and undergrowth, rather than push it. She followed Staines at a slower pace, her breath rasping in her throat.

When she arrived at the den, Staines was holding back some springy branches that served to disguise the entrance and Lucy pulled the wheelchair through, unceremoniously pulling the skirt of her dress free from some thorns that had snagged hold of it. She turned round, surprised to find herself no more than a few inches away from Lord Rockhaven's standing figure.

'Oh!' She let go of the wheelchair handles and instinctively stepped back a little. 'You're standing. It … it seems strange.'

Lord Rockhaven was holding on to an overhanging branch with his left hand and his face was taut with controlled pain. Bruno lay at his feet, his body relaxed but his eyes watchful. A faint flicker of a smile relieved the tension of Lord Rockhaven's face. 'Yes. I have improved much in the past few weeks, but I cannot yet walk unaided.'

He held out his right hand and Lucy found herself responding to his gesture by placing her right hand in his.

'I have much to thank you for,' he said tenderly, looking down into her eyes. 'I hope to have the opportunity another time to thank you more leisurely.' Glancing down, he turned her hand until it was palm uppermost and looked at the scratches and the blisters that were already forming. He traced the lines of scratches tenderly with the pad of his thumb, then looked up again, his one eye revealing a depth of emotion that made Lucy's heart race with anticipation and she held her breath as he lifted her hand up to his lips and tenderly kissed her palm.

She would not have believed that such a simple act could have such an effect on her heart. It was beating so rapidly within her breast that she quite expected it to burst out of its confines. His action was more moving than any of the well-presented protestations of undying love that many of her suitors had effusively uttered. She felt a warm blush flow over her cheeks and she lowered her eyelashes in confusion, not wanting him to see her reaction to his courtly gesture.

'Tell me your full name, so that I may greet you properly the next time we meet,' he asked softly.

'L-Lucy Templeton,' she stammered, feeling almost dizzy from her close contact with this man. She raised her head slightly and her glance settled on his lips; lips that curved into a lazy sensuous smile that seemed to invite her confidence and promised ... what? She wasn't sure, but she hoped she had the chance to find out. She knew what those lips felt like; their smooth velvety strength had teased her own lips into a yielding spiral of desire. A kiss completely forgotten by its giver, she realized.

Time seemed to stand still and she couldn't tear her eyes away from his face. In spite of the scar and the patch over his eye, his expression was … tender, she realized. Her thoughts led her to run the tip of her tongue lightly over her lips and they tingled in anticipation.

Impassioned by the simple action, Lord Rockhaven groaned within himself. How he wished he had met this entrancing young woman before he had been injured so disfiguringly! He sensed she might have been the one who could have banished the blackness of the family curse that had hung over him since his childhood.

By the softness of the hand that he still held, he realized she must be of genteel birth, maybe a poor relation of some local family. He vaguely thought of the Cunninghams whose land was separated from his own by this small woodland. Of course, that's why they felt free to play there! There had been no children in the family in his younger days, but, now that his thoughts took him this way, he remembered Cunningham's pretty but compliant wife who had graced his mother's drawing room on several occasions some years ago. Was she the mother of the children who had accompanied Miss Templeton on their first meeting? They had called her Aunt Lucy. Was she Mrs Cunningham's sister? Or, from the lack of style in her clothing, a more distant relative?

Whoever or whatever she was, she was no namby-pamby socialite! She had as much courage and resourcefulness as a seasoned campaigner on the Peninsular and he wanted to know her better. But not now. Not while his cousin's presence in the area might endanger her life along with his own.

A small cough brought them both back to reality.

'The young lady'd best be on 'er way, Cap'n,' Staines warned. 'We've no knowing what Lieutenant Potterill might be doin'.'

Lord Rockhaven released her and unsteadily regained his balance, shaking his head in wonder. He wasn't sure what had happened within him. Was she aware of his thoughts? He looked at her searchingly, wondering if she would be looking at him with loathing for having lifted her hand to his lips.

She wasn't. Her eyes steadily held his and she seemed to be as spellbound as he was. She wasn't repelled by him: her face glowed with wonder.

He felt a jolt of— He wasn't sure what to call the sensation he felt as he looked into her eyes. He suddenly knew that, if he survived the coming encounter with his cousin, he would come back and search her out – whatever her social standing, or lack of it; she had pierced his heart.

He reached out and gently trailed his fingers down her cheek. 'Thank you,' he murmured softly. 'I am indebted to you, but now you must go.'

'Yes,' Lucy said faintly, pulling her thoughts together. 'I … I'll come back in the morning, if I may,' she whispered faintly. 'To make sure you're all right,' she added, as if fearing that her motive was likely to be misunderstood.

He gripped her hand again, holding it tightly in the intensity of his sudden fear for her safety. 'Do not return tonight, nor, if you suspect that Piers is still here, tomorrow. He would have no hesitation in eliminating you if he thought you privy to his actions. Promise me!'

Lucy felt a pang of fear. This was no game they were

playing. Her startled eyes met Lord Rockhaven's intent gaze.

'I demand your promise!' he insisted, all traces of softness now gone from his expression.

Lucy nodded. 'I promise,' she whispered. She withdrew her hand from Lord Rockhaven's and made herself smile briskly. She knew she had to be on her way – her presence was a hindrance to his concealment – and she was anxious to be somewhere on her own so that she could sort out her tumbling emotions.

'God be with both of you,' she said, as she carefully slipped out of the den between the overhanging branches and hurried back to where she had left her gig.

'A grand lass,' Staines commented, as the branches dropped back into place. 'What I'd call a real lady.'

'Yes,' Theo agreed, thinking of the softness of the hand that had lain in his, burning his own toughened skin. 'Lucy Templeton,' he repeated softly, knowing he would be forever in her debt. But, there was no time for such reflections right now – he had all night for that!

'Help me into the chair, Staines,' he said more briskly, 'then you, too, must be on your way. And, yes, may God go with you, my good friend.'

Nine

L UCY REACHED HER gig, relieved that the remaining dog was barking no more than its usual recognition of her presence. She swiftly unhitched Maud's reins and led her round to face the track before she climbed aboard. Then, with a click of her tongue and a gentle flick of her whip she signalled Maud to set off. She felt tense with apprehension, thinking that, for once, she would be relieved to be back at Glenbury Lodge, and even more relieved on the morrow when she met Lord Rockhaven once more and was assured of his safety.

She had seen a softer side of his nature, the part of his character that would have been more evident to his mother and grandmother, generating within them the obvious love they bore for him. Had he been aware of the surge of passion she had felt for him? She hoped not. She had worn her heart on her sleeve too visibly when she had thought that Mario Vitali was as much in love with her as she had been with him. And how mistaken had that belief been! But not even that sobering thought could dispel the euphoria that surrounded her. She felt as though she were floating on air. 'Oh, please keep him safe!' she breathed in almost silent prayer. Surely, tomorrow they would be laughing about a wasted piece of drama!

She paused at the end of the track and drew in her breath sharply. A well-appointed curricle was coming at a fast pace from the direction of the village. The hope that the vehicle would continue past her faded as the curricle slowed its pace. The driver, a dandy if ever she saw one, regarded her with an aggressive air as he began to turn his matching greys towards the track.

She immediately knew from Mrs Boulton's description that this was Lord Rockhaven's cousin. Someone must have indeed mentioned the vagrant ex-soldier to him and he was coming to check who it was. She had to delay him!

Clicking her tongue and giving the reins an imperceptible flick, she urged Maud forward. The man's aristocratic features glared down at her as he realized that a collision was imminent.

'Hey! Look out!' the man bellowed, pulling hard on his reins.

Lucy tugged on the left-hand rein, swiftly followed by a tug on the right, giving Maud a contradictory signal. Maud mis-stepped and, instead of turning, reared slightly as she found herself too near the high-stepping greys.

At that point, Lucy put the best of her driving skills into practice and pulled the left rein again, taking Maud to within a whisker of the off-side grey and her gig followed behind, her wheel neatly sliding between the curricle's off-side wheel and the body of the curricle.

A sharp oath briefly drew her glance to the thickset groom in the rumble seat, his weatherbeaten face snarling at her seeming ineptitude. A ripple of fear ran down her spine but she concentrated on reining in Maud before irreparable damage was done to her gig.

The dandy had brought his greys to a shuddering halt. They were now rearing and bucking, their eyes rolling wildly at the sudden halt to their progress. The man uttered a coarse oath as he strove to control them. Lucy's face flushed with embarrassment and anger, but she strove to keep her voice in neutral tones.

'Oh, dear,' she uttered mildly, looking up at the irate driver, hoping that he took her rosy cheeks to be the outcome of embarrassment. 'We seem to have become entangled somewhat, don't we? I'm most dreadfully sorry.'

'Entangled? You clumsy—' He managed to bite back whatever epithet he was about to bestow upon her and, instead, ground out, 'Ham-fisted drivers such as you should be barred from driving on public roads. If you were a man I would knock you from your seat! Get down at once so that we can sort this mess out – and keep that bone-setter still, will you!'

Lucy felt incensed. Even though she had performed a deliberate piece of bad driving, she couldn't believe that any gentleman, even one of dubious character, would speak to a woman in such a high-handed fashion. Her mouth tightened as she fastened the reins to the side of her seat, then stood and swung around to face the furious young man, the backs of her hands resting on her hips.

'Maud is no bone-setter, sir,' she said indignantly. 'She is as finely bred as your … your …' No, not even in anger could she pour scorn on his beautiful pair. She decided to change tack and use feminine wiles. 'Well, maybe not,' she said in softer tones, 'but she is a sweet goer, all the same. I beg you, sir, do not blame my pony for my mishandling of her.'

'"Mishandling" is not how I would describe your lack of driving skills, miss,' he said haughtily. 'Do you realize that you could have caused a nasty accident here? I have never seen such appalling driving, even from a female!'

'I *did* avert a bad accident, though, didn't I?' Lucy challenged. 'You were driving so swiftly, I felt sure you were about to sweep us off the road. And I am sure your man can readily sort us out.' She decided a bit of flattery might help her cause. 'I confess I was lost in admiration of your greys,' she declared, imitating the breathless tones that she recalled some of her fellow debutantes using when wishing to sweet-talk a suitor, and fluttered her eyelashes in a beguiling manner. 'The sight of them quite took my senses away. But then, I am sure that you must be used to such a reaction as mine. However, I do apologize, sir.' She lowered her head and then looked up at him coquettishly from under her lashes, another action she remembered scornfully witnessing at a ball one evening.

'Hmph! I suppose it could have been worse,' he allowed. 'However, you'd best get down so that Hodge can get to work on sorting it out.' He had already secured his reins and he leaped down on the far side of his curricle as he spoke, joining his man, Hodge, who was appraising the interlocked wheels.

Lucy climbed down from her driving seat and stood on the grass verge, watching as the two men worked to persuade Maud to back up a couple of steps to separate the two wheels without causing damage to the curricle.

It took only ten minutes or so and Lucy decided that some effusive thanks would secure a few more moments of delay. She clasped her hands together at her breast as Lieutenant Potterill approached her, fastidiously wiping his hands on a linen cloth.

'Oh, how clever you are! What a good thing it is that men

are so much stronger than we females. I don't know where we would be without you.' She flashed him a winsome smile and saw that her praise mollified him somewhat, though he didn't answer her. His hand cleaning complete, he looked her up and down disdainfully and obviously decided that she was far inferior to his class.

'Your gig is ready. Be on your way,' he said dismissively, 'and learn to handle your pony more skilfully before you risk other people's lives again!'

Lucy suppressed the indignation that rose within her and assumed an expression of humble gratitude. 'Yes, sir. I thank you kindly.' She bobbed a slight curtsy and turned towards her gig.

'Wait a moment.' His eyes narrowed as he said suspiciously. 'What were you doing coming from Montcliffe land? I suppose you know you have been trespassing?'

Lucy decided a bit of spirit wouldn't go amiss. His attitude really was insufferable. She drew herself up and met his superior glance with a hauteur of her own.

'Although I see it as no business of yours, sir, I have been on a charitable errand. After hearing that an unfortunate ex-soldier who has been discharged without a pension has taken residence in the old cottage in the wood, I have taken him some wholesome food.'

'Really?' His eyes gleamed with a sudden interest. 'Er, what sort of man is he, this ex-soldier?'

Lucy forced some lightness into her voice. 'Exactly what you would expect an ex-soldier to be – a capable but disillusioned man struggling to put his life back together.'

'Indeed?' His eyebrows rose perceptibly. 'But what class of man? One similar to myself, would you say?'

Lucy regarded him coolly. 'Oh, no, sir. A little lower than you. More like your groom, I would say.'

His lips tightened. Lucy might have smiled if she hadn't felt so tense. As suspected, he had no sense of humour.

'How many men are there?' he asked sharply.

Lucy injected a tone of surprise into her voice. 'Only one man is there,' she replied carefully.

He looked at her appraisingly, as if weighing up her answers. It took all of Lucy's nerve not to wilt under his hostile glare.

'And where are you going now?'

'That, sir, is none of your business. But, as it happens, I am going home.' She hoped she had given Staines enough time to get back to the cottage and dismantle the parallel bars and whatever other actions he needed to do to erase any evidence of Lord Rockhaven's recent presence there. 'Good day to you, sir.' She nodded her head curtly in his direction before abruptly resuming her driving seat. 'Giddy-up, Maud!'

Her hands were shaking as she flicked the reins – indeed her whole body was shaking. Her skin felt as if a thousand pins were being pricked into it and she knew without doubt that the man was still watching her departure. However, she refused to give him any sense of satisfaction by looking over her shoulder. The longer he delayed moving on the better! She only wished she might have been able to witness his disappointment when he saw the man in question wasn't his cousin.

Lucy returned the pony and gig to the stables and hurried inside, knowing that she had spent more time away than she usually did. What a blessing it was that this had happened whilst Marissa and her family were away. Her longer absence would not have escaped her sister's notice and she would have been compelled to explain the reason. Fortunately, Cook was readily side-tracked with Lucy's volunteered information of how the villagers appreciated her culinary gifts and she affably bade Lucy to get up those stairs and change for dinner.

Lucy spent an anxious evening. It infuriated her to know that if she were a man, she could creep back through the wood to see what was happening and maybe be of assistance if Lieutenant Potterill did indeed have the evil intentions Lord Rockhaven suspected of him. She blew out her candle and kneeled on the window seat at her open bedroom window, staring into the darkness towards the small wood-land. She listened intently through the still night air and heard an owl hooting in the distance, but nothing more. What was happening out there? Was Theo safe?

She let his given name swirl around in her thoughts ... it suddenly seemed so natural to think of him as such. Her heart was in turmoil over him. How could she have changed in such a short time? She recalled the old dowager countess asking, 'Would you marry him, Miss Templeton?' and her heartfelt answer of, 'No, not unless I loved him.' How impossible that had seemed then!

But, now? Even though she had seen so little of him, her feelings towards him had dramatically changed. She felt ... what was it? A racing excitement when she was with him and the same when he was in her thoughts, but she had little hope that he felt the same. She felt he had built an impenetrable wall around his emotions, but he *had* held her hand and kissed her palm. Surely that meant he had some feeling towards her? Or was it just gratitude for her assistance?

Her thoughts sobered and concern about the outcome of the next few hours swept over her. Had Lord Rockhaven's cousin taken Staines's word that only he was living at the cottage? Had he driven off? Returned to the Eagle and Child for the night? Would he return the next day to search further? She would have to visit Mrs Boulton again and get her husband to try to find out what Lieutenant Potterill's plans were. Or had Potterill somehow discovered Lord Rockhaven's hiding place and was he, even at this moment, lying injured – or worse – alone in the darkness? No, Staines would not have allowed that to happen. He would have given up his life for his master!

Her breath caught in her throat. What if he had? It would have been two against one, with evil intent an added weapon in Potterill's hand.

Oh, how could she just sit here as though nothing were amiss? But she had promised not to return. She bit her lower lip. Did such a promise override her desperate concern for his safety?

Even now, Lord Rockhaven might be at Lieutenant Potterill's mercy! But, if that *were* so, she knew her presence would more than likely make the situation worse. She *had* to leave it to Lord Rockhaven and Staines. Oh, but it was hard to remain here not knowing!

'Theo ... Theo.' She rolled his name over and over and then whispered aloud, 'Theo ... be safe!'

*

She was awake with the lightening sky and waited impatiently until she knew her early appearance wouldn't cause too much comment. After hurriedly partaking of some breakfast, she changed into her carriage dress once more, hoping that its tears weren't noticeable and presented herself in the kitchen.

'I must make a return visit to – to one of the homes I visited yesterday,' she told Cook, her fingers crossed in the fold of her skirt. Her actual words could be taken as truth but she knew her intent was to mislead and it didn't sit easily with her. 'One of the sons is … er … ailing and I promised to return today. Some bread and milk would ease their situation and … er … anything else that can be spared.'

'Now, don't you be getting too involved, Miss Templeton,' Cook warned. 'Charity is one thing, but too much can lead to problems. I'm sure your sister didn't intend you to spend quite so much time visiting the village, nor should you be visiting this early. Tell me who it is and I'll send Nora with one of the grooms.'

'Oh, I'm quite happy doing what I'm doing,' Lucy assured her. 'I would be riding that way anyway and I'm sure my sister would approve.' If ever I am able to tell her, she added silently.

Cook shook her head doubtfully, but she had already organized her staff to cover certain tasks that day. Eeh, and what would be the harm? She doubted Mrs Cunningham would be interested in the fine details of Miss Templeton's activities as long as no scandal was attached to them. And charitable giving was the good Lord's command, wasn't it? So, she set to and made up a basket of food suitable for an invalid.

Lucy hurried to the stables. As requested on her return the previous day, Maud was already harnessed to the gig and Lucy was able to set off to discover what, if anything, had happened overnight. She knew Wellington would enjoy a run but decided his behaviour was too unpredictable and his presence could be a liability. She must get Theo to show Bertie how to discipline him more effectively ... if only he was still safe!

She turned into the track towards the cottage, her heart beating rapidly. What if Lieutenant Potterill were still here? Even the parcel of food would be a poor excuse for such an early visit.

She need not have worried. When she reached the place where she could see the outline of the cottage faintly through the trees to her left and where the narrower track into the wood went straight ahead, all seemed quiet. At the same moment, she heard a dog barking in the distance ahead. That meant Theo must still be in the children's den. Was Staines with him? He must be as he or the second dog would surely have heard her approach if they were in one of the outbuildings. As she urged Maud to proceed forward carefully, Bruno burst out of the bushes and bounded towards her, still barking and baring his teeth.

Her heart almost froze with fear at the sight of him. He was a large dog and, right at this moment, seemed ferociously powerful. He was more than capable of leaping up at her on the driving seat of the gig if he so wished. She reined Maud to a standstill and said tremulously, 'Good dog, Bruno! I'm a friend, remember!'

He put his front paws upon the edge of the seat and thrust his muzzle at her, still growling, though not as fiercely as a few moments ago. It took all Lucy's self-control not to jerk herself away. 'Good dog!' she repeated and hesitantly held out her hand for him to sniff. 'Good dog. Do you remember me? Where's your master? Is he all right?'

She knew he couldn't understand her words but, from what she had witnessed the previous day, he was an intelligent dog and would sense that she was no threat to him and his master. He seemed to do so. His tongue hung from his mouth as he panted no more than a few inches from her face.

'Where's your master?' she repeated. 'Find him! Find Theo!' He must still be in the den, she reckoned, since she was sure Bruno would have stayed with his master until he heard or sensed her approach. But why hadn't Staines taken Theo back to the cottage? Was he at the den with his master? Her anxiety increased. She glanced towards the cottage. It was the nearer of the two but her main concern was to see if Bruno would lead her to Theo.

She remembered the command Theo had given him the previous day. 'Patrol!' she said sharply and pointed deeper into the wood. To make her own intentions clear, she flicked her reins to tell Maud to move on and, as the gig moved forward, Bruno dropped back to the ground and barked at her.

'Go on! Find!' she commanded. Bruno bounded off in the direction of the den and Lucy guided Maud more slowly behind. The undergrowth was getting thicker and the ground softer. Lucy knew she couldn't get the gig much closer. Maud was already finding it difficult to pull the gig forward and Lucy decided to stop whilst she could still turn the gig around. She pulled on the reins and jumped down and then led Maud in a circular path so that she was facing back the way she had come, thankful that it was easier to move the gig without her weight in it. She tethered the reins to a low bush and then looked around.

Bruno was watching her, his body ready to move on.

'Go on. I'm coming.'

She lifted up the hem of her skirt and began to work her way through the bushes and undergrowth. Bruno bounded ahead and she could hear him not far in front of her. The tone of his bark had changed and she wasn't all that surprised when she came upon the fallen figure of Lord Rockhaven.

'Oh, no!' She ran forward and dropped at his side. She could tell that he had been pulling himself along the ground but, although he looked dishevelled and grimy, he didn't seem to have been harmed in any way. His face was grim with pain and anxiety.

'I thought it must be you coming,' he said tersely without preamble. 'I hoped it was, anyway. Can you help me to get up?'

'I'll try.' She stood up and leaned over him, wondering which part of him to seize hold of. 'Are you all right? What happened? Why didn't you wait for Staines to come for you?'

Bruno began to lick his master's face. Theo pushed him away and then pushed himself up so that his upper body was clear of the ground. He tried to tuck his left leg under him so that he could prise himself upwards, grunting as he did so, 'I fear for Staines's wellbeing and that of my other dog, Solomon.' Perspiration ran down his face but the effort was beyond his capabilities and he sank back to the ground. 'Help me roll over,' he commanded. When he was lying on his back he added, 'They would have been here by now if either were capable of doing so. Here! Try to haul me to my feet.' He held out his left hand but Lucy was unable to haul him up, no matter how she stooped and braced herself.

'These blasted legs of mine!' he cursed in fury. 'I'm useless!'

'Shall I go to the cottage to see what's happening there?' Lucy asked hesitantly. She was doubtful she would find Staines and Solomon in fine health.

Lord Rockhaven obviously had the same thought. 'No!' he said sharply. 'I'll get up somehow.'

'Where's your wheelchair?'

Theo let himself sag back into a sitting position. 'Back there. I tried to hold on to it but the ground is too soft. When it fell over, I decided to try to pull myself along the ground but I haven't made much headway.'

'Right! Stay there! I'll go and get it. We might be able to make use of it between us.'

Lucy darted into the bushes and came upon the wheelchair about 200 yards back, not far from the den. She righted it and then tugged it backwards to where Lord Rockhaven was waiting. She marvelled that he had got so far crawling along the ground. No wonder his clothes and hands were in such a filthy state.

'Now, all we have to do is get you upright and holding on to the chair,' Lucy said optimistically.

That was easier said than done. There was no way Lord Rockhaven could pull himself upright, even with the help of the chair, not even with Lucy sitting in it to give it stability. Perspiration ran down his face.

'It's futile!' he ground out between his teeth. 'You'll have to leave me here and go and see what has happened to Staines. I'm sure no one is there or Bruno would be letting us know.'

Lucy didn't want to leave him. He was so vulnerable on the ground.

'One more try,' she said, casting her eyes around. 'I know! If you can crawl to that tree and somehow pull yourself up by it, I can get the chair behind you. It's not far from the path and I'm sure I could pull you along there as far as my gig.'

It wasn't easy and, by the time Theo was able to drop back into the chair, his hands were badly lacerated from dragging himself up the tree trunk with them taking his weight. Pulling him backwards in the chair over the soft woodland floor was hampered by Lucy stepping on to her skirt each time she took a step back.

'I'll have to take it off!' she cried in despair. 'Otherwise, we'll be all day.'

Theo hated the position he was in. It was bad enough when Staines was wheeling him about but this was far more degrading – yet this courageous girl hadn't uttered a word of complaint. She amazed him! He didn't know her exact position in life, but he knew she was no country village girl. Her hands were too soft and her language too genteel. Nor could she be of his social class. Most women he knew would be horrified by his disfigurement and his inability to even get to his feet. Yet Lucy Templeton just got on with it, almost as if his crippled state was the natural way to be. She was even prepared to disrobe herself in order to get on with the task in hand. He wished more men in his company had been half as resourceful.

'You don't have to do that,' he said aloud. He twisted around to look up into her flushed face. Lord, she was beautiful! 'I'm sure you won't take this amiss, but the women who followed the army used to somehow tuck their skirts up out of the way. I don't want to sound indelicate, but if you push the front of your skirt back through your legs and pull the back part forwards, you should be able to tuck the end in at your waist. That will keep it clear of the ground.'

Lucy felt her face flush, but he was right: it was no time to be delicate or missish. She let go of the handles of the chair and tried what he had suggested.

'Like this?' she asked eventually, stepping forward.

He nodded. 'Exactly like that.'

It felt almost as she had imagined wearing trousers must be like, and had often wished she had been born a boy instead of a girl. How stupid society was to insist that girls wore full skirts and layers of petticoats – such impractical clothes for country pursuits!

She grinned, partly to cover her embarrassment. 'How sensible,' she declared.

It was still hard work, but she was able to make progress and once they were on the narrow path, it was much easier. Even so, she was greatly relieved when she reached her gig. Her arms ached – her whole body ached – but they weren't home and dry yet. She let down the tailgate of the gig and, with Lord Rockhaven using the strength in his arms and Lucy placing his legs in the right position, with much pulling and pushing, he eventually lay sprawled in an undignified manner on the floor of the gig.

'There's some bread and milk in that basket,' she told

him, as she climbed stiffly up on to the driving seat. 'That will help you regain some strength.'

It was only a few minutes back along the track to the turn-off for the cottage. Bruno had scampered ahead and had rushed around the cobbled yard, nose to the ground. He now stood barking outside the door of the outbuilding. Lucy wondered why there was no response from Solomon. She drove as close to the outbuilding as she could and, as she jumped down from the gig, a glance in the dog pen showed her why Solomon was silent: his body lay amidst a pool of blood. She felt sick. His throat had been cut.

She looked away, unable to bear the sight. But it was no time for feminine weakness. The whereabouts of Staines was the main problem and she took a step towards the outbuilding.

'Help me down!' Theo demanded. He, too, had seen the body of his dog and his face was taut. He didn't want Lucy to be the one to discover Staines's body.

Lucy hesitated. She knew what was in his mind. Bruno was alternately barking and whining, his nose snuffling at the lower edge of the door.

'Do as I say!' Theo commanded.

Lucy went to the rear of the gig and let down the rear rail. Using her shoulder to support him, Theo managed to stay on his feet as he slithered out of the gig. She climbed up into the gig and lowered the chair down beside Theo and held it steady as he seated himself in it.

'Right! Let's see what's what!' he said grimly. He wished he could spare her this, but he knew he couldn't physically manage it on his own. 'Open the door and push me in.'

It took a short while for their eyes to adjust to the dim

interior but, before that happened, they knew from a throaty groan that at least Staines was still alive, even though badly injured. He lay sprawled on the floor, his face bloody and his body twisted in an unnatural position.

'We need help,' Lucy declared as she knelt beside him. 'I can't move him and neither can you. He's lost a lot of blood. He'll die if we can't stop the bleeding.'

'He'll die if we leave him,' Theo said just as firmly. 'Go and get some water and look for some clean cloths. The cleaner we get him, the better chance he'll have.'

Lucy found a pail of water in the cottage and used a knife to tear up her petticoat into strips of cloth. Under Theo's instruction, she cut open Staines's jacket and shirt to find where his injuries were, washed them as best she could and then bound them with the strips of cloth. He had multiple knife wounds, but they seemed to have missed vital organs. Staines groaned throughout her ministrations but was barely conscious. His body was badly bruised and his right leg was twisted at a peculiar angle – Lucy knew it was broken – and what was left of his right hand was a mess of pulped flesh.

'Stamped on and ground into the floor,' Theo said tersely, seeing her puzzled stare.

Lucy felt faint. She had never seen such injuries. She was exhausted. She sat back on her heels and wiped her hand across her face, pushing her hair out of her eyes. Tears streaked her face, though she didn't realize it. Theo reached out and stroked his thumb across her cheek.

'Well done, my little one,' he murmured. 'I think you've done all you can for now. He needs a doctor, but it's too far for you to go in your gig. Who do you know who can be trusted implicitly? Who are your family? What about them?'

'They are away, visiting Lady Somerfield in Kent. There are a few servants left behind. I think they would be loyal to you, but I can't be certain. I think I know someone in the village … a Mrs Boulton, who speaks well of your mother.'

'Is Georgie Boulton related to her?'

'Her husband.'

'Good. He'll do. Tell him to go to Dr Fortesque and request that he comes here as soon as he can … tonight would be better but I daren't leave Staines unattended until then. Tell him to ask the doctor to bring a suitable carriage. Swear him to secrecy and tell Boulton to make sure my cousin has left the area, and to make sure he isn't followed, especially when coming here. When he's done that, ask him to choose someone entirely trustworthy to bring with him, but not to let anyone else know what he is doing. The fewer who know, the better.'

'Where will you go then? It isn't very safe here.'

'I haven't quite decided yet. I need to think things through carefully. Now, before you go' – his voice dropped, edged with tenderness – 'dip that cloth into some clean water and hand it to me.'

Lucy did so, wondering what he wanted it for.

Theo smiled. 'Lean down a bit. A bit closer. That's it.' He reached up and gently wiped her cheeks and across her forehead. 'That's better.' He smiled and it lit his features. 'Wash your hands and then tidy your hair. You look all in. Are you sure you are up to going to the village? I wouldn't ask it of you, but there's no other way.'

'I'll be fine. Where shall I leave you until help gets here?'

'I'll stay here with Staines. Bruno won't let anyone get close without warning me and, just to be extra sure, would you mind opening that cupboard over there? That's right. Carefully hand me the pistol you should find within. Thank you. Now, if you'll move me into that corner behind the door, I'll be able to see anyone who comes in before they see me.' He gave a hard laugh. 'Better warn Boulton to come in carefully!'

'May I come back? After I've seen the Boultons?'

'Better not, for I have no doubt that Piers will be back. He murdered my brother and has seriously harmed my good friend. He has gone too far to leave it there, but, next time, I will be ready for him.'

He took hold of her hand and Lucy wondered if he was going to kiss it again, but he didn't. He held it for a moment and stroked his fingers along its length a few times.

'Take care, Miss Lucy Templeton and, as *you* said yesterday, may God go with you.'

'And may He stay with you,' she whispered, as she straightened her body. Her throat felt too tight to say more and she hurried away, anxious to complete her allotted task, hoping she didn't meet too many people who might wonder at the state of her.

Ten

LUCY ENTERED THE village with her senses alert, determined that, if Piers Potterill were still in the area, she would know it. Her frequent visits throughout the past week or so had made her presence accepted without query and she received a number of cheery acknowledgements. However, unsure whether or not her physical appearance would stand up to too close a scrutiny, she didn't stop until she reached the Boultons' cottage.

'Eh, miss! Whatever—?'

Lucy held up her hand, cutting short Mrs Boulton's exclamation of surprise. 'May I come in, Mrs Boulton? I know I seem rather dishevelled but I need your assistance … and that of your husband. Is he available?'

'Eeh, bless yer, miss, he's harvesting at Gerard's farm. Shall I send fer him?'

'Please, but say nothing to alarm him or anyone else. Just say something like he is needed at home.'

'I'll send our Johnny. He's a fast runner. Now sit yer down, miss, and let me mek you a cup of tea, an' I'll get a brush fer your hair, miss. Eh, whatever has happened? You look fair done in.'

Lucy briefly told her as much as she felt necessary and

let the concerned woman make her a little more tidy. Later, when Georgie Boulton hastened in, his face flushed with his exertions, she repeated the tale.

'I be honoured to help 'is lordship, miss, and don't fret none. I know any number to choose from to give a 'and. Now you get yerself back to yon lodge, miss, and put yer feet up. Leave it to us men. We'll see to 'is lordship, and sort yon upstart out, we will, or my name's not Georgie Boulton.'

Lucy was thankful to return home. Cook was curious about her long absence, but Lucy made the excuse that she had spent her time with Mrs Boulton and hadn't been aware of how long she had been there. She was glad Mrs Boulton had helped her to tidy up her appearance and Cook seemed unaware of the stains on her carriage gown. She knew her sister would notice the stains and tears and resolved to get it brushed and sponged down before Marissa's return ... but not today. She was too tired to work out a strategy to avoid too many questions.

Not that Cook was completely blind to the irregularities of Lucy's behaviour. 'I'll be glad when the master and mistress are back and no mistake,' Cook now admonished her, with the familiarity only an old family retainer would dare to assume. 'You young folk today have far too much liberty. It didn't happen in my day, I can tell you! Young ladies knew what was expected of them, not like today!'

Lucy tried to look suitably chastened and asked for a tray to be sent up to her room before making her escape, thankful that she didn't have a maid to make excuses to, though she was sure Susie would have relished the excitement of her last few hours.

She sighed at the state of her hands as she slipped out

of her dress. They were scratched and blistered and felt quite sore. She slipped into Marissa's room and borrowed a pot of her rose-scented salve, knowing she wouldn't mind. When she was little, Marissa used to enjoy dressing her up in her nice clothes and letting her try out her creams and powders, painting her face and curling her hair, until Lucy tired of sitting still. Ten minutes later, she would look more like a ragamuffin than the daughter of a peer of the realm unlike Marissa who never had a curl out of place and had never ever torn her dress! They were totally unalike, but they had been very close and attached to each other until Marissa's marriage took her away from the family home.

Smiling at childhood memories, Lucy changed into a comfortable day dress, then lay on her bed and gently applied a lavish amount of the delicately perfumed cream to the palms of her hands, reflecting over the events of that day.

She had known a mixture of terror, excitement, despair over her lack of physical strength and satisfaction that she hadn't handled the situation too badly. Oh, why were women so restricted in what they were allowed to do! If she were a man, she would still be there, making plans with Theo and making sure that Piers got his just deserts.

Her thoughts sobered. Piers Potterill had shown himself to be a ruthless adversary. Would that give him an advantage over Theo, who, she was certain, wouldn't stoop to any dishonourable act? What would Theo decide to do after he had moved Staines to a place of safety? How could he get the better of his cousin without coming to any harm himself? In a fair fight, she was sure he would win, but

Piers had shown himself to have scant regard for honour and chivalry. He wouldn't wait until they were standing face to face. He had already shot both brothers in the back and then denounced them as cowards! She was sure his next attempt would follow similar lines.

Lucy felt a rising indignation against him, but it was a helpless fury. She was only a female and was relegated to the sidelines, out of danger when all she longed to do was to fight at Theo's side. An image of them standing side-by-side, swords at the ready, slipped across her inner vision.

Oh, he must come through it the victor! She couldn't bear it if he were hurt, or worse. Right must prevail! She suddenly knew that she wouldn't want to go on living if anything happened to him. Life would have no meaning.

At that moment, Theo was thinking through a series of plans to ensure the same outcome. The first thing was to get Staines assessed by Dr Fortesque and, hopefully, transferred to a suitable place for his recovery. He was confident that the good doctor would remain faithful and discreet. He had seen him and Con through many boyhood ailments and mended broken limbs on occasions. Maybe Fortesque would take Staines to his home? Thankfully, money to pay for any treatment was no problem. As long as they could transfer Staines there without anyone realizing what was happening, he should be safe.

He turned his thoughts to his own predicament. What would Piers do next? He tried to put himself in his cousin's role. Would he come back here to the gamekeeper's cottage? Or was he now persuaded that he had been mistaken about Theo's presence there? Had he visited the Hall and found it closed and shuttered? Theo hoped so. That might send him back to London for a time to follow other lines of enquiry, which would give *him* time to come up with a plan and put it into practice.

His eyes gleamed. There was nothing like a challenge to restore feelings of self-worth. And, at least he knew his enemy! Piers was a cheat, a liar, a murderer, a thug and a bully and, like most bullies who got others to do their dirty deeds, he was a coward. That knowledge was the ace up his sleeve. If he could get Piers into a tight corner, he would react in the only way he knew and, with reliable witnesses to backup his testimony, Theo would have him!

By the end of the day, Theo knew what his immediate plans were: Dr Fortesque needed no persuasion to take personal care of Staines and Boulton and Dodds, Boulton's chosen ally, were prepared to take on Staines's work and assist Theo in his efforts to get his legs working again, but in a location neither would know until they had taken leave of their families.

His only regret was that he couldn't tell the two women in his life where he was and what he was doing. One of those women was his dear mother, the Countess of Montcliffe and the other was Miss Lucy Templeton, whose assistance and bravery he would remember for the rest of his life.

Lucy was devastated when she discovered that Lord Rockhaven had departed for a secret destination. Her only consolation was that he had taken Georgie Boulton and another villager with him, with the intention, so Mrs Boulton told her in strictest confidence, of regaining the use of his legs and eventually coming back to his ancestral home.

'But when will that be?' Lucy asked Mrs Boulton, her heart in despair.

'Georgie couldn't say, love. It seems his lordship is determined to keep his plans close to his chest and what we don't know, we can't let slip, can we?'

'But how will you manage without your husband bringing in a wage? I know things were difficult before, but it will a great deal harder on your own.'

'Georgie said his lordship has got it all in hand. Old Tomkins from up at the Hall will take care of our needs. So, Miss Templeton, we just has to be patient and see what happens.'

That was easier said than done. How could she be patient when she didn't know what was happening, nor how long it would be before she saw Lord Rockhaven again? If ever! The thought drove her to despair. He hadn't said he wanted to see her again. Maybe, now that her part in his survival was over, he would forget about her? After all, what was there for him to remember? A slip of a girl who spoke her mind too freely and romped about the countryside with little thought for her reputation. What sort of enticement to him to keep her in his thoughts was that?

It was a subdued Lucy who, a few days later, welcomed her sister and family back home from their visit to Kent and Marissa wrote happily to their mother, saying that the isolation from society was having a good effect on her sister's rebellious nature. Lady Templeton wrote back with thankfulness and said that they would leave Lucy with Marissa until Christmas, when they would travel down

from London to spend the festive season at Glenbury Lodge
and take Lucy back with them early in the new year in time
to plan a second Season, during which, Lucy would be
prevailed upon to receive the first favourable offer of
marriage with thankful gratitude.

Wisely, Marissa did not share this plan with Lucy. She
just hoped that her rebellious sister had seen the foolishness of her former romantic notions and, now that she had
had a glimpse of what her life might be like if she remained
unmarried, that she would resolve to be a dutiful daughter
in future.

Lucy knew that Bertie and Arabella would be eager to
ask if they might visit Rocky at the earliest opportunity and
she managed to interrupt Bertie's urgent enquiry of, 'How's
Rocky? Can we go and—?' with a hasty, 'The stable pups are
all doing fine, Bertie, but you must wait until tomorrow
morning to see them,' thankful that Cassie had indeed
produced a litter during the children's absence. Her interruption was accompanied by a meaningful raised eyebrow
and she was thankful that Bertie was quick on the uptake.
Her conscience twinged with guilt that she was teaching
the children to be deceitful, but she salved her misgivings
with the knowledge that Lord Rockhaven's safety took
precedence over the normal niceties of life.

The following afternoon, after taking the children to see
the new pups, she tried to explain the difference between
lying and using an untruth to protect someone's safety. 'We
aren't lying for selfish gain for ourselves, or to escape a
punishment,' she clarified, 'and we will be able to confess
the truth to your mama as soon as Lo— Rocky says we
may.'

Bertie considered her words. 'That's all right, and I'll be very brave if I get a beating for having told a lie.'

'Will I be beaten, too?' Arabella asked with a tremor in her voice.

'Nah! Girls don't get beaten, do they, Aunt Lucy?' Bertie asserted with a hint of scorn in his voice, adding hopefully, 'Maybe Rocky will say I, too, may be excused for once, because we were lying to protect him? I'll ask him, shall I? Can we go and ask him now?'

Lucy crouched down so that her face was level with the children's faces. 'I'm sorry, children. Rocky had to go away quite suddenly. Er ... Mr Staines was taken quite poorly and they have gone away to make him better. It's only for a while and I'm sure they will return before too long.'

'But, where've they gone? Can't we go to visit? I'm sure he'd like us to,' Arabella asked.

Lucy shook her head. 'I don't know where they've gone. We just have to wait until he comes back, or lets us know where he is. I'm sure someone will tell us eventually.' She fervently hoped so.

The children looked crestfallen and Arabella slipped her hand into Lucy's, both giving and receiving comfort.

'I bet Rocky's sailing the seven seas, searching for treasure ships!' Bertie declared optimistically, raising the edge of his hand to his eyebrows as if he were searching distant horizons. 'I hope he comes back when I'm a bit older, then I can go with him. I'd better practise fighting and catching prisoners and making them walk the plank! Come on, Bella, you can be my first victim!'

With shouts and squeals, the children happily diverted into another make-believe game and Lucy suddenly felt quite ancient in comparison to their innocent acceptance that, eventually, all would be well.

'I pray that it is,' Lucy breathed silently. 'But when? When will Lord Rockhaven return? Will I still be here?' She couldn't bear to think that she might not be. If she weren't, maybe Lord Rockhaven would forget all about her, as he had done after their first brief meeting, and that was too heart-wrenching to even contemplate!

Theo was equally frustrated. His self-imposed regime of fitness-training was arduous.

His first task for Boulton and Dodds was to retrieve the dismantled exercise bars that Staines had constructed for him. Not wanting to risk anyone deducing that he was in residence in the servants quarters at Montcliffe Hall, he planned the operation with military precision, instructing his two faithful cohorts to temporarily conceal each separate piece in different parts of the woodland, making it difficult for anyone who might catch sight of any part of the proceedings to keep a watch and lie in wait for the next move. He made use of the extra time this entailed in making their living quarters more habitable, aided by Tomkins, the elderly retainer left as caretaker of the family home when his mama had removed to Town.

Once the pieces of equipment were reassembled, his twice-daily exercises began in earnest. He gritted his teeth and persevered, even when his muscles and ligaments were screaming for rest and sweat was pouring down his forehead. Boulton and Dodds now knew better than to suggest a break before Theo was ready to give in to his protesting body. He had set himself a goal and was pushing his body hard to reach it. He knew that his next meeting with his cousin Piers would more than likely be the final meeting one that would end with a victor and a loser.

He knew that when he had set himself on this course of just retribution, he hadn't really cared if his own life was forfeited, but he felt differently now. When his spirit flagged or his progress seemed to be non-existent, it was a certain pretty face that came into his mind and urged him to persist with it.

He wasn't sure when his feelings towards her had changed from irritation at her presence to sensing a loss when she was absent. In the cold dark hours of night, when aches and pain racked him, he despaired that his war-torn body would ever be anything other than a deterrent to any young lady wanting to pursue a closer relationship with him, but, in the clear light of day, when he experienced minor steps forward in his progress towards physical fitness, he exulted in the memories of Miss Templeton's gentle concern and total lack of any sign of abhorrence at his bodily weakness and facial disfigurement. Could he dare hope that she might learn to have some—? His thoughts jerked to a standstill – he dare not hope for love, but maybe, if he were allowed to court her, some feelings of tenderness might develop towards him?

But, first, he must become fit enough to face his cousin, if not on quite equal terms, at the very least, on terms that allowed him a chance of victory. Conrad deserved nothing less.

By the time the leaves were falling from the trees in late October, Theo knew he was gaining ground. His muscles were strengthening, his endurance increasing and the

intermittent pain in his back almost negligible. He practised swordplay but knew his impaired mobility would
forever disadvantage him in that sphere and determined,
instead, to use pistols in his avenging of Conrad's death.
This time, *he* would call the tune, not Piers! He would
choose the time, the place and the means, allowing Piers
the dignity of a face-to-face confrontation, not a cowardly
shot in the back followed by a kick in the face when he was
down!

As the time for retribution drew nearer, knowing that his
cousin would never attempt to face him on his own, but
would shield himself behind a number of paid assassins,
Theo instructed Boulton and Dodds to carefully recruit
more like-minded men from the village, trusting their judg-
ment about who would remain loyal under fire.

At last he was ready. He had regained his physical
strength; he had his plan of action and the men to support
him, and the advantage of intimate knowledge of the lie of
the land. All he needed to do was choose the date and time
and then dangle the bait before his cousin.

A few weeks later, in late November, the Countess of
Montcliffe was sitting in front of her dressing-table under
the administering hand of her maid, when there was a
discreet tap at her door.

Lady Montcliffe's eyes met with her maid's and a slight
indication of assent sent her maid to open it.

'A letter for m'lady,' Dutton, the butler, murmured
quietly.

Lady Montcliffe's heart leaped, though whether in joy or
terror, she wasn't sure. All she knew was, for Dutton to have

brought the letter up to her door himself, it must be of some importance – and the whole household knew the sole cause of the state of anxiety their mistress was in! It *must* contain news of Theo! But was it good news or bad? Her face was pale and her hand trembled as she reached out to take the franked folded paper from the silver tray her maid was now holding towards her.

Although she felt, deep within her heart, that her remaining son was still alive, there were moments when she feared otherwise. Surely, he would have communicated with her before now if he were able to do so? He must know that she was almost driven out of her mind with worry about him. She only had to glance into a mirror to see what effect his long absence had had upon her. Only her maid's skill with powder and paint had enabled her to face Society's enquiring gaze with a modicum of self-assurance, and to cope with her odious nephew's persistent and insincere enquiries as to whether or not his dear cousin had at last been in touch with her. He was even getting credit to fund his opulent lifestyle on the expectations of his imminent inheritance, if the circulating *on-dits* were to be believed.

Lady Montcliffe's lifelong training in well-bred deportment made her involuntarily straighten her shoulders and, although she almost feared to take the letter, she did so unaware that she was holding her breath, and forced herself to read its handwritten direction. Her left hand flew to her breast and her heart leaped with joy as she recognized the hand that had scribed it. It was from her dear Theo! At last!

Oh, she had known that if he were still alive, he would

eventually get in touch with her, and now he had! He had contacted her at last. Her face glowed with happiness. Oh, where was the dear boy? How was he faring?

She slipped her finger under the seal and eagerly began to read. The first words were, *Dear Mama, if anyone is with you when you receive this letter, delay reading it until you are on your own.*

The countess immediately dismissed her maid, asking her to inform the servants not to disturb her under any circumstances until she rang for them. She was definitely not at home to visitors.

She eagerly resumed her reading. Theo didn't go into many details of what he had been doing since he left her shortly after his discharge from the military hospital, except to say that he had been adequately cared for and was now much stronger and was looking towards reopening Montcliffe Hall for Christmas.

What I want you to do, Mama, is to begin to make arrangements to return at that time ... BUT I want you to make sure that my cousin Piers 'accidentally' overhears that I will be returning there on my own in the family coach the second Friday in December, expecting to arrive by late afternoon. Dispatch the coach to arrive on that date, laden only with such luggage as it might be supposed I would need to take with me and tell Simkins to be sure he is protected against the hazards of such a journey in winter.

Do not worry, Mama. If all goes to plan, we will be reunited before Christmas.

Your loving son
Theo.

In Lady Montcliffe's heart joy at her son's recovery and her imminent reunion with him warred with anxiety over his immediate safety.

'Oh, Theo, what are you planning to do? How can I *not* worry? Do be careful!' she whispered aloud.

Eleven

A T THE END of the first week of December an air of excitement began to circulate in the village. A number of them, all former servants of the Montcliffes, had been recruited to give the Hall a thorough cleaning and an army of outdoor labourers began to tidy the grounds under the orders of Thornley, the previous head gardener.

It was Peggy, the upstairs maid who had brought a jug of hot water to Lucy's room for her morning wash, who excitedly told Lucy that her mam and da were well pleased.

'Da's had to get work wherever he could since her ladyship left,' she confided to Lucy, 'but now he's hoping to get taken on full-time again. It'll make heaps of difference.'

'Is it known who is returning to the Hall?' Lucy asked carefully. 'Is it just her ladyship? Or is Theo ... er ... Lord Rockhaven coming as well?'

'I dunno, miss. I 'spect we'll find out soon enough. Oh, isn't it loverly, though? It's said her ladyship will be back before Christmas.'

Lucy agreed. She was sure Marissa would allow her to visit Lady Montcliffe if she were still here when her ladyship was back in residence and, hopefully, she would then discover what Lord Rockhaven's plans were.

Knowing that gossip was likely to be rife in the village, she offered to take some provisions to the villagers that afternoon whilst the children played under their mama's watchful eye. She ended her round with Mrs Boulton. That good lady drew her inside her cottage with an air of suppressed excitement.

'I shouldn't be saying this, miss, but I knows you are as loyal to the family as we who has known them all our lives, but my Georgie has let me know that he will be home any day now! By the end of next week at the latest. Ain't that wonderful, miss? He'll be with us afore Christmas!'

Lucy's heart leaped with anticipation. 'Indeed, it is wonderful! Does that mean Lord Rockhaven is coming home also?'

Mrs Boulton touched the side of her nose knowingly. 'Georgie didn't say, but I know my Georgie well enough to know he wouldn't be coming back wi'out him.'

'Let me know if you get to hear anything definite, won't you, Mrs Boulton, *especially* if anything is seen or heard of that man who came here before?' She was sure Theo's cousin would not have given up his plan to become the next Earl of Montcliffe, but, if she was able to do anything about it, he wouldn't succeed.

The following Friday morning, Lucy awoke with a sense of excitement. Marissa was taking Bertie and Arabella to a pre-Christmas party at the home of some neighbouring gentry and Lucy was not included.

'You know I would love to take you along, Lucy,' Marissa had apologized on receiving the invitation the previous week, 'but Mama insisted that you must not be allowed to attend any social functions until she says so and it won't be long now until she and Papa come to stay for Christmas. I am sure she will relent when she hears how good you have been. You aren't too disappointed, are you, dear? I know Arabella especially will miss you.'

The imp of mischief that invariably sat on Lucy's left shoulder made her grin impudently. 'We needn't actually *mention* it to Mama, need we?' she suggested slyly, thinking of all the other undeclared violations of her mama's orders that had occurred during her time of 'exile from home and society'.

'Lucy! How can you say so?' Marissa exclaimed, her expression as shocked as her tone.

'Did you *never* disobey Mama?' Lucy asked curiously, then answered her own question. 'No, I don't think you did. Did you never even *want* to do so?'

Marissa seemed genuinely puzzled by the question. 'Of course not. Mama and Papa always know what is best, besides, you did enough rebelling for the two of us.' Her expression softened. 'Oh, Lucy, I used to be in such a quake over you and often cried myself to sleep after you had been punished, but you never seemed to mind your punishments and you always bounced back straight afterwards.' She reached out a hand and touched Lucy's arm. 'But, Lucy, you will heed Mama from now on, won't you? You've managed to be good all the weeks you've been here and it wasn't so very hard, was it?'

Lucy was so touched by her sister's obvious concern that it was almost on her tongue to confess her misdeeds. Only her sworn promise to say nothing to anyone about Lord Rockhaven's recent sojourn in the area constrained her. 'I'll do my best,' she promised honestly, 'but I can never be as compliant as you, dear Marissa. As to whether I am disappointed not to be included in the party invitation, I am a little, but I know what Mama said and I am quite happy not to be included. Don't upset yourself about it. I know Cook is making up some charity baskets with special Christmas treats in them for the villagers, so I will make good use of the time and distribute some of those.' And, hopefully, get to hear the latest news that might have reached the faithful villagers regarding Lord Rockhaven, if neither he nor lady Montcliffe has returned by then, she added in her heart.

She had been on tenterhooks throughout the week, but no one in the village seemed to know anything more definite other than one of the Montcliffes was expected to be back in residence before the end of the week.

Now the last day had arrived, she bounded out of bed, swiftly dressed and hurried downstairs to breakfast with her sister. Since their parents were due to arrive the following day, the house was filled with a hum of activity and Marissa was already presiding over the informal breakfast table, determined to personally oversee the maids as they performed their routine cleaning tasks with extra diligence – a decision that wasn't altogether approved of by Mrs Hardy, her housekeeper.

Lucy greeted her with a sisterly peck on her cheek and helped herself from the array of foods kept under covers on the sideboard ... some tea, two poached eggs and a slice of grilled ham. Fresh baked rolls of bread were in a shallow wicker basket on the table with lovely cool curls of butter on a silver platter.

'The coffee is quite fresh,' Marissa commented, as Lucy

sat down opposite her. She picked up a folded note from a plate which a footman had placed at her side and broke the seal of the hand-delivered note. 'Oh, that's a nuisance!' she declared petulantly. 'The Misses Treddam have finished the new carriage dress I am giving you as your gift for Christmas, but both have severe colds and cannot bring it here for your final fitting. I did want it to be ready for when Mama and Papa come tomorrow, for your other one is a perfect disgrace and I cannot for shame allow them to see you so shabbily dressed. I really don't know how you have got it in such a state, Lucy. It looks as though you have romped in the woods in it!'

Marissa wasn't far wrong, Lucy reflected ... but knew it wouldn't be circumspect to say so. She composed her features into as innocent an expression as she could. 'We could go *there*, couldn't we? I haven't been into town whilst I've been here this time and it would give me the chance to purchase a few Christmas gifts for the children, wouldn't it?'

'That's not possible! It would need to be done today in case it needs some alteration. You surely haven't forgotten that I am committed to taking the children to visit the Darlingtons this afternoon and they live in quite the opposite direction! Bother!'

She tapped her fingers impatiently on the table, as she ran through her plans for the day. 'I suppose you could go by yourself,' she murmured hesitantly. 'I can't let you have the town coach, though, since Taylor is conveying me and the three children and Nurse Harvey in that. You'll have to use the barouche. With its hood up and warm rugs to cover your knees, it will suffice. And you can have Higgins in attendance,

Taylor says he is doing well under his tutelage, and Nora could go as your abigail. She is eager to learn the duties such a position entails – and her parents live in town, so she could pay them a visit whilst you are having your fitting. Yes, I'm sure Mama would find no fault in such an arrangement. It is hardly a social call, after all, is it? … Oh, dear!'

Another complication had occurred to her and an expression of consternation puckered her face. 'I cannot allow the Misses Tredham to see you in your tattered carriage gown. I know, you must wear my second-best one. I find it tight around my waist at the moment but, apart from that, thankfully, we are much of a size. There! The problem is solved, Lucy.'

Lucy's initial reaction was of disappointment that she wouldn't be able to make use of her free afternoon to visit Mrs Boulton in order to learn the up-to-date news of Lord Rockhaven, as, surely, he and Lady Montcliffe must be coming any day now, but she swiftly saw that the expedition to town needn't disallow a visit to the village on her way home so she eagerly fell in with Marissa's suggestion.

As soon as lunch was over, Lucy left Bertie and Arabella in the care of an undermaid and she hastened to her room to change into Marissa's carriage gown. It was a deep russet brown, a colour that suited Marissa more then herself. She posed in front of the cheval-glass, turning from side to side, reflecting that, although it was slightly loose around her waist, the style suited her slender figure. It had a matching bonnet with a feather that curled around the brim and perched quite cheekily on top of her head. With matching gloves and a small reticule dangling from her wrist, she felt pleased to be dressed once more as a member of the *haute ton*.

'My trouble is I want the best of both worlds,' she spoke to herself, thinking how she also enjoyed romping through the wood in her oldest clothes and, with a last approving glance at her image, she went downstairs, where Nora, one of the junior maids, awaited her.

Their groom, Higgins, had the barouche ready waiting for them at the front steps. He had only recently been promoted from more lowly stable duties and, resplendent in his new uniform, was pleased to be have been chosen to drive the mistress's young sister into town. The stable lads were more aware of Miss Templeton's irregular escapades than his master and mistress were and they regarded her with a mixture of reluctant disapproval that a young lady of her class should so freely flout the laws of convention and admiration that she readily did so! They also knew of her frequent trips to the village during the mistress's weeks of absence and recognized her genuine concern for the welfare of the struggling village families.

Consequently, when Miss Templeton, looking as pretty as a picture, lightly tripped down the front steps in the wake of a junior footman, followed by Nora, a maid for whom he felt quite a fancy, his breast swelled with pride. He managed to maintain his polite impassive pose until Miss Templeton was seated within the barouche, but risked tipping Nora a cheeky wink as she scrambled up the step behind her and was rewarded by a pretty blush and a toss of the maid's head, an air of *hauteur* that was lessened by a gratifying sparkle in Nora's eyes.

The footman folded up the step and slapped his hand against the carriage, the command to depart. They were off!

Under normal circumstances, it would have been an uneventful drive, but to Lucy, it was her first proper outing since her arrival five months ago and she felt greatly liberated. Nora, intent on showing that she deserved her chance of promotion, knew better than to take liberties with Miss Templeton's easy manner, but, nonetheless, quickly relaxed and responded readily to questions about herself and her family and her hopes of promotion, and a comfortable camaraderie was soon established between the congenial pair.

In answer to a question regarding her family, Nora confided, 'Me mam and da run The Red Fox, a tavern in the middle of town, miss. I used to help out there, but when I got the chance to work for Mrs Cunningham, me mam decided I must take it. Our Dottie and Edna do my work now. I can't wait to see what they think of my smart uniform! Did Mrs Cunningham tell you I'm allowed to visit them while you're getting your dress fitted?'

'Indeed she did, Nora. I don't know the exact layout of the town. Will it be practical if I am first taken to the Misses Tredham's establishment and then you can direct Higgins to your parents' tavern?'

'It's only across the road and down a bit, miss,' Nora agreed with a giggle. 'He can't miss it. How will I know when you're ready for me to come back to you, miss? Mrs Cunningham said I've to look after you at all times.'

'The Misses Tredham will send a message to let you know,' Lucy assured her, smiling at the girl's eagerness to do everything properly. 'And then, you'll be able to show me where I can buy some suitable Christmas gifts, won't you?'

'And can I tell me mam that you'll pop in to say hello to her?' Nora asked ingenuously. 'She'll be ever so pleased to see what a fine lady I'm working for ... and Dottie and Edna'll be green with envy!'

Lucy laughed. 'Yes, I'll "pop in" to say hello. Now, it seems we have arrived. Higgins will come round to lower the step. He will hand me out first and then you may follow. Come inside with me so that all proprieties are kept and then come back to the carriage. Higgins will wait for you, and then you can pretend that it's *your* carriage and draw up at your parents' tavern like a grand lady.'

'Ooh, miss! I'll send Higgins inside to fetch them out. I bet their eyes will pop right out!' Nora's face glowed with merriment and both were still chuckling at the thought when Higgins opened the carriage door and lowered the step and assisted Lucy to descend gracefully on to the narrow paved footpath.

She stood still and looked around, making a sigh of contentment. She was enjoying this afternoon of freedom. But she must remember not to delay too long in town: there was the other important matter to attend to.

The two spinster sisters welcomed her into their provincial parlour. Sniffing delicately into their handkerchiefs, they fussed and twittered and directed their underlings in the fitting of Miss Templeton's carriage dress and showered extravagant compliments upon her, but they were talented at their jobs and Lucy felt delightfully elegant in the royal blue carriage dress that they had made for her. It fitted her to perfection. With a matching bonnet perched over her curls, a fur-trimmed muff to warm her hands and a pretty reticule dangling from her wrist, she twirled and posed in front of the many angled mirrors that showed every aspect of her trim form.

She couldn't help wondering if maybe Lord Rockhaven would feel more attracted to her if he saw her thus dressed? She knew he probably thought her to be nothing more than a hired servant, or a poor relation at the very best. Well, if he really were returning before Christmas and Lady Montcliffe took up residence at the family home once more, surely the Cunninghams and Templetons would be invited to share in at least one dinner party. She knew Marissa was fondly hoping so, and, just as surely, her mama would not let pass an opportunity to parade her daughter before such an illustrious peer of the realm. Her face glowed at the thought.

But, first, he had to get here safely and re-establish himself in his proper and rightful place without the threat of his cousin's machinations hanging over him.

So, she must conclude her business in town and then go to the village to discover what news she could glean of Lord Rockhaven's return.

With the new carriage gown and all the accessories conveyed to The Red Fox by a liveried servant, Lucy was reunited with Nora and they spent the next hour gazing into shop windows and deliberating over ideas of what to buy as her gifts to family members and close servants. Her choices made, neatly wrapped parcels were piled in Nora's arms as the maid excitedly followed Lucy from establishment to establishment, smiling delightedly as she received compliments from shopkeepers she had known all her life but never had the means to even enter their shops.

At length, with her purchases completed to her satisfaction, Lucy suggested they return to The Red Fox to partake of light refreshments before returning home.

'Yes, miss. Mam said she'd lay aside her best parlour for you and Dottie an' Edna are going to serve you. Higgins and me'll have something in the kitchen. Mam's ever so pleased I'm doing so well. I'll tell 'em you're here, shall I?'

Nora ran ahead and disappeared through the side door of the tavern. Lucy hesitated on the threshold, unsure whether to proceed or not. She had never been into a town tavern before. Her only experience of such places was when she had been travelling to or from home and then only in the company of her mama and numerous servants, when she had simply followed where they had led. Her limited experience made her aware that young ladies of her class did not enter such places unaccompanied and, quite frankly, now she was faced by the dim interior of the tavern, she didn't know which way to go.

Hearing voices from behind a closed door, she tentatively pushed the door open but her body froze into immobility as a portion of the smoke-filled room came into view. She immediately realized that the room was occupied by men only and most of its occupants were garbed in the sombre colours of the lower classes, their voices rough and untutored. She knew that such a room was not for the likes of herself and made to draw back before she was spotted. Her withdrawal was halted when the back of a figure previously hidden by the door stepped partly into view.

It was his many-caped coat and the outline of his head as he arrogantly tossed a coin on to the table where the other men were sitting that first caused her to pause and, for one hopeful moment, her heart leaped as she thought it was Lord Rockhaven himself. But the over-cultured voice as he said, '... and there's more of the same for any man looking for a good night's work!' made her silently draw back, for it wasn't Lord Rockhaven at all.

It was his cousin, Lieutenant Piers Potterill.

Twelve

LUCY COULDN'T BELIEVE Potterill was so convinced that he was above the law! But it seemed he was! He was either very sure of himself or very foolish. Lucy hoped it were the latter.

'And what sort of work would that be,' one drinker was saying as Lucy listened silently.

'Work that any man worth his salt should be able to do with little effort,' Potterill loftily responded. 'As long as he's willing to keep his mouth shut!'

Lucy's swift intake of breath caused the man to swing round to face her, his expression darkening as his gaze rested upon her. Lucy felt a stab of alarm. Would he recognize her from their previous encounter? Hopefully not, since she was now dressed in her sister's fashionable gown and bonnet.

She decided to play with an innocent air and, forcing down her fear, she flashed a charming smile around the small room.

'I beg your pardon for disturbing you, gentlemen. I seem to have lost my maid, but I can see she isn't in here. Do excuse me.'

She made to withdraw but Lieutenant Potterill swiftly

strode towards her and grasped hold of the door to prevent it from closing. Lucy took a step backwards and Potterill reached out a hand to restrain her. 'Not so fast, ma'am! I don't take kindly to people eavesdropping on my conversations! What is your business here?'

His grip on her wrist was hurting and Lucy tried to control the fear that was once more rising within her. His daring to touch her caused a spurt of anger to surface and she used it to her advantage. She drew herself upright and forced herself to look him straight into his eyes, letting her anger be known.

'I have already apologized for my interruption,' she said coldly. 'Please let go of my wrist. You have no need to restrain me.'

'I will be the judge of that!' he snapped. 'I ask again, what is your business here?'

Lucy held his gaze and his hold of her slackened a little. She decided to try to disarm his suspicions and allowed her stance to relax slightly as she said a little ruefully, 'It is as I said. My maid is new. She stepped ahead of me, no doubt thinking to clear the way of any unwelcome attentions to my person but I was too dilatory in following her. I have never been here before, nor have I ever entered any such hostelry unaccompanied. As you can see, there are numerous doors in this corridor and I tried the first one to hand.' She gave a deprecatory laugh. 'I found the darkness a little unnerving, sir, as I am sure you can understand.'

Potterill's hard glare relaxed slightly and the thin line of his mouth twisted into the start of a sneer at her feminine apprehension. It caused Lucy to react with resentment at his poor opinion of her femininity, a reaction he didn't miss and he tightened his grip once more, his brow puckering in concentration.

'Have we met before, ma'am?' His eyes narrowed as he studied her face. 'I feel we have and I very rarely forget a face.'

Lucy's alarm grew. She didn't want him to connect her in any way with his cousin. 'I am sure I would remember *you*!' she retorted spiritedly. 'I am not used to such cavalier treatment!'

'Aren't you?' His tone was slightly sarcastic, but he seemed to respect her refusal to be cowed by his treatment of her. 'Then perhaps you should be more careful where you place yourself. Young ladies who wander unaccompanied into places such as this should expect to meet with, shall we say, a lack of the usual courtesies you would meet with in a drawing room.'

His lips parted in what he might have supposed to be a smile but, to Lucy, it seemed more threatening than placatory. Their eyes locked once more and her movements froze for an instant.

A sound behind her made her jump and she quickly glanced in the direction of the sound and was vastly relieved to see Nora's face looking anxiously at her.

'Ah, there you are, miss!' Nora spoke with evident relief. 'I thought you'd got lost, miss. Mam ses will you come this way?'

'Thank you, Nora. I am coming immediately.' She faced Potterill again, her chin held a fraction higher than before. 'Good day, sir. My presence is required elsewhere.' She jerked her wrist and this time he released her. Then, just as swiftly, he caught hold of her hand and raised it to his lips.

Lucy couldn't suppress a shudder and hoped he put it down to maidenly innocence.

'I look forward to our next meeting, Miss—' He paused enquiringly. 'I don't recall you sharing your name?'

Lucy pulled her hand free. 'No, I didn't,' she responded haughtily. 'I feel under no obligation to do so. Good day, sir!' And she quickly followed Nora through the door that led into the front part of the hostelry, aware that she was shaking inside.

As Nora ushered her forward through the door into a much lighter part of the inn, Lucy's mind whirled over the alarming encounter with Theo's cousin. What was he doing here? Did he know Theo was returning? Was he planning to waylay him? If so, how much did he know? Did he know the exact date of Theo's return? Was it today? Or tomorrow? She needed to find out more.

Nora led her to a small but pleasant room that over-looked the street in front of the tavern. A round-faced woman who was waiting there bobbed a small curtsy as Lucy entered.

'Please be seated, Miss Templeton, and make yerself at home,' the woman bade her. 'I'm Nora's mam. Me and Joe are right glad you've done us the honour of coming under our roof and letting our Nora pay us a visit. Our other daughters'll fetch you a tray of tea and buttered scones when you're ready and Joe'll pop in to see you when he has a minute but he's a bit busy with other customers right now.'

'Thank you, Mrs Roper.' Lucy sat down but her head was whirling. What could she do? How could she find out more about what Potterill was planning? Did she dare trust Nora's parents? But what could she say? What could she ask of them that wouldn't betray too much of Lord Rockhaven's confidences? Would they be loyal to a man they mightn't really know all that well? A man whose reputation had been recently besmirched?

They weren't local to the Montcliffe estate and she didn't know enough about them to know if she could place her trust in them. They would probably regard it as a bit of female hysteria. No, she must think about it calmly before taking anyone in to her confidence. They mightn't think it worth the risk of displeasing a customer.

But Higgins might! His family lived in the village and some of them possibly had worked on Montcliffe land and, more than likely, hoped to do so again. Surely he'd have some loyalty to the family? She'd have to risk it.

She forced herself to stay calm and smiled warmly as she peeled off her gloves. 'Whilst I am waiting, Mrs Roper, I would be obliged if I might have a word with my groom?'

'Of course you can, miss. He's supping a pint of ale in the kitchen. Nora, go and tell the lad to come here … and tell our Dottie and Edna not to keep your mistress waiting. Get on, now. We've other customers to see to, as well … I begs yer pardon, miss.'

Mrs Roper bobbed another small curtsy and bustled out in Nora's wake. It wasn't long before an anxious-looking Higgins presented himself in the parlour. He touched his forelock and mumbled, 'I'm sorry, Miss Templeton. I thought it'd be all right if I only had one pint.'

'Pardon? Oh, your drink of ale. No, that's all right, Higgins. What I want is something entirely different. Tell me, honestly, what are your thoughts on the Montcliffe family? Are you looking forward to their return to their home?'

'Eeh, I am that, miss. We all are.' Higgins response was swift, though he looked puzzled. 'They'll soon get things up and running again, miss. They'll see us all right, like they always have in the past.'

'Good. There's something I want you to do for me, Higgins. Something important, but you mustn't let anyone realize what you are doing. There's a man … a gentleman … talking to some local men in the back room out there. I fear he is up to no good. Can you somehow listen to what he is saying and what the men say in return? And then come and let me know? It's very important.'

'Yes, miss. I already took a tray of their drinks in, to help out, like. I'll offer to take another, shall I?'

'Yes, do that. And quickly, before he finishes his business and goes.'

Higgins left and was soon replaced by Nora's two younger sisters, both smartly scrubbed and giggling nervously at each other as they bobbed hurried curtsies and placed their trays on to the table. Lucy had two pennies ready for them and they bobbed another curtsy as they grabbed the pennies and backed out of the room.

Lucy really felt too nervous of what Lieutenant Potterill might be planning to have much appetite but the scones looked appetizing and almost melted in her mouth. Her compliments to her hostess were genuine when it was time to leave. She hoped Higgins had completed his mission without drawing attention to himself. Had he learned anything important?

As Nora slipped quietly back to her side, she whispered conspiratorially, 'Higgins is back outside, miss, and he says the gentleman 'as gone.'

Higgins was waiting by the side of the barouche, the step already down. He looked around quickly before saying, 'It seems no one took the gentleman up on his offer, miss, and he's left in a huff. Whatever he wanted, no one here was willing to do it for him.'

Lucy didn't know whether to be glad or sorry. At least if someone had agreed to the offer, she might have had the chance to find out what Potterill had in mind. 'Right. Thank you, Higgins.' She paused with one foot on the step. 'I would appreciate it if you say nothing whatsoever about what has just happened to any of the other servants, Higgins. Nor you, Nora. I just know that that man is an enemy of Lord Rockhaven's and he is planning something bad, but I don't know quite what.'

She climbed into the barouche and Higgins waited until Nora had joined her before lifting the step and closing the door. Lucy was still troubled. Times were hard for common folk. There were always some who would sell their souls for gold and if Lieutenant Potterill looked hard enough, he would eventually find someone willing to help him in whatever dastardly deed he was planning. The fact that he was back in the area showed he knew Theo was returning soon … and Theo wouldn't know! His life could be in imminent danger: she must, somehow, warn him!

'Are you all right, miss?' Nora enquired anxiously.

Lucy managed a faint smile. 'Yes.' She didn't want to talk. She needed to think. 'I'm just a little tired, that's all.'

'It was a lovely outing, miss. Mam and Da were right pleased to meet you. Did I do all right for yer, miss? Will you tell Mrs Cunningham?'

'You did very well, Nora, and yes, I'll tell Mrs

Cunningham how efficient you have been. But I think I'll close my eyes for a moment.' She knew there was little point going to the village now. Potterill surely wouldn't have the effrontery to try to recruit accomplices from there and the afternoon was passing by. It would be dark soon. If Theo or Lady Montcliffe were planning to return today, maybe he or she was already there. Unsuspecting targets.

Since Potterill was hiring men to assist him in whatever foul deed he was planning, it must be happening soon. He wouldn't want to give the men time to change their minds or inform the authorities about it. It must be tonight. Or tomorrow at the very latest.

She wondered if she should ask Higgins to drive on to Montcliffe Hall so that she could make proper enquiries, but she didn't know if anyone there would be in a position to do anything about it. And, if she did, what would she say? She had nothing to speak of save a growing unease about Lord Rockhaven's safety.

But that unease was growing. Surely Theo's safety was the most important thing. What was the threat of punishment compared to that?

She knew immediately what she must do. She must risk telling Marissa what it was that she feared. She would have to tell her all about it, right from the very beginning and hope she would understand. And, if Rupert were there, *he* could initiate an enquiry at the Hall. She felt Theo would understand if, by her anxiety on his behalf, she inadvertently committed a social blunder. As long as it was handled discreetly.

She almost smiled. When had she started to worry about

doing things discreetly? The word didn't used to be in her vocabulary.

'We're nearly home, miss,' Nora's voice penetrated her inner musings.

'Mmm. Thank you, Nora,' Lucy murmured. 'Ohh!' Her eyes flew open with a start as the carriage lurched over to the left and both she and Nora were flung from their seats into a tumbled heap on the floor. Ouch! Lucy's head banged against the hard wood of the doorframe and the next few moments became a bit hazy. Sounds of panic from the horses merged with the sound of splintering wood as the axle of the carriage was dragged along the road and it seemed as though the juddering and shaking was never going to stop.

When, at last it did stop, there was an unearthly stillness that seemed all the more alarming and, for a few moments, Lucy felt paralysed in mind and body. What had happened?

She opened her eyes to discover she was in a topsy-turvy world. The roof of the carriage sloped down to her left and both she and Nora were half under the rear facing seats. Above their heads was the seat she had been sitting on; now it was leaning over her at a drunken angle.

One of the horses neighed and must have attempted to move forwards because the carriage lurched again.

'Miss?' Nora's voice seemed petrified.

Lucy forced herself to think clearly. They needed to get out whilst they could do so, in case the horses panicked and caused even more damage to the carriage. She moved her arms and then her body. Although she felt bruised, every-thing seemed to be working satisfactorily and she struggled to extricate her legs from where they were jumbled with Nora's. At last she was able to sit up.

'Can you move, Nora?'

Nora struggled beside her. 'I … I think so, miss. Ooh, my head hurts! I didn't 'alf give it a bang!'

She gingerly touched the back of her head and Lucy leaned forward to feel it also. 'I can feel quite a bump forming, Nora. No doubt it will be the size of a goose egg in no time at all …' – she drew back her hand – 'but there's no bleeding. My nursemaid used to say, "Where there's no blood there's no lasting damage". I'm not sure it was always correct, but it lessened my desire to cry, so we will believe once more. Now, it doesn't seem as though anyone is coming to help us so let's try to get ourselves out of here.'

They managed to disentangle themselves and, by standing on the edge of the rear-facing seat and grabbing hold of the looped strap that hung down from the far doorframe, Lucy was able to reach up and force open that door. It wasn't easy and she felt quite exhausted when at last the door flopped forward and clattered against the side of the carriage.

'I'm going to try to clamber out, Nora. Be ready to take my hand when I am able to reach down for you.' Lucy was thankful that she was no namby-pamby miss. Her sister may have despaired of her tomboyish ways but they were standing her in good stead right now.

When the two girls were balancing precariously on the sloping top of the carriage, Lucy could see that they were only yards from the entrance to Glenbury Lodge and, when she looked around to see if anyone was in the vicinity to help them, she saw Higgins limping along the road about twenty yards behind them. She realized he must have been flung from the driving seat when the carriage first became unstable. He was lucky to be alive.

With all three of them shaken but at least on their feet, Lucy directed Nora to make her way to the house and Higgins to calm down the horses.

'Use the front door, Nora. It is the nearest. Farrell will organize the men to come to our aid. And, no, don't worry about the parcels,' as Nora seemed to be a bit bewildered and was more concerned with scooping up some of the scattered parcels than obeying her directions. 'Farrell will see to them too and have them taken upstairs. Then, get yourself off to Mrs Hardy to let her know what has happened … and ask her to assure Mrs Cunningham that we aren't badly hurt. I will come as soon as someone else is here to help Higgins with the horses.'

Higgins was already holding the two bridles and talking in soothing tones to the two horses. He had a bloodied gash across his forehead and, from the way he winced each time the horses pulled against his hold, he was in some degree of pain. He looked relieved to hand one bridle over.

Lucy began to talk to the horse as she gently stroked her free hand down its nose. 'There! There! Everything's fine!' she murmured. She glanced at Higgins. His face was quite pale under the streaks of blood and dirt that besmirched it. 'Do you know what happened, Higgins?' she asked, as much to distract him from his present discomfort as for want of information.

'Don't rightly know, miss. T'front wheel just came off. Though I checked everything afore we left t'yard. There was nothing wrong with the wheel then. Summat must 'ave loosened it!'

'Or some*one*?' Lucy mused out loud.

'Yer what, miss?'

Lucy compressed her lips. The less she said the better at this stage, since her thoughts were only guesswork. 'Thankfully, you were driving with extreme care, Higgins,' she complimented him instead. 'Things could have been much worse if you had been driving more recklessly.'

Higgins seemed shocked by the insinuation that he might have been likely to drive with less care. 'Eeh, no, miss. Mr Taylor would 'ave me guts for garters if he thought I'd put your life at risk!'

Lucy laughed at his words, though the action brought a stab of pain. She was feeling a little light-headed, wasn't sure how much longer she could hold on to the horses.

Help was at hand. A shout from behind them alerted them to the approach of a number of the outside staff and stable hands, followed a little more decorously by Farrell and two underfootmen. Lucy was more than thankful to hand over to them and only made a murmuring protest when Farrell insisted that the two footmen made a chair of their joined hands to form a seat to carry her indoors.

Now that dealing with the carriage accident was in other capable hands, Lucy dragged her mind back to the urgency of her concern over Theo's return and Lieutenant Potterill's probable treachery and, as Farrell instructed the footmen, 'Take Miss Templeton upstairs', Lucy twisted around and said, 'No, no, Farrell, I need to speak to my sister or Mr Cunnigham. It's very important.'

'I'm sorry, Miss Templeton, that's impossible. Mrs Cunningham and party are not yet returned from their afternoon visit. I believe it is to go on until early evening … a special treat for the children.'

Lucy's face fell. 'Oh!'

She hadn't realized. That was a blow. What now? How was she to seek to warn Theo about his cousin's presence in the area? She was almost sure that he had somehow engineered the interference with the wheel of their carriage which meant he must have recognized her from their previous encounter and deemed her a possible hindrance to his plan. Her heart chilled as she realized that, with no more than a suspicion of her complicity, for it could have been no more than a suspicion, he had been willing to put not only *her* life at risk, but also those of her two servants. A man so ruthless would stop at nothing to gain his objective.

She must *do* something!

Thirteen

LUCY KNEW SHE could not involve her sister's servants in her desperate plan to warn Theo or his servants about Potterill's presence in the area. They would be unlikely to act upon her say-so and would probably feel compelled to persuade her to wait until her brother-in-law returned home later, but *later* might very well be *too late*.

As her agitated mind raced over her options of how she could proceed, her glance flickered about the reception hall. She spotted an unopened franked letter on the silver platter on the hall table and recognized her mama's hand. Much as she loved her parents dearly, she hoped all this intrigue was over before they arrived on the morrow, or, at least, her warning passed on. It spurred her on to come to a decision, reflecting ruefully that her mama would have hysterics and probably faint if she knew what her younger daughter was now contemplating.

'Think calmly,' she told herself. 'First things first.' She needed to ensure that she was left undisturbed for the rest of the evening. She halted the progress of the two footmen who were about to ascend the wide staircase with her still seated upon their entwined hands and spoke to the butler. 'Farrell, will you send word to Mrs Hardy to attend me in my room?'

'Certainly, Miss Templeton. She will be with you directly. In fact, here she is right now.'

Mrs Hardy was hurrying along from the back of the house, her usual calmness overtaken by a natural agitation at the unfortunate event of the overturned carriage.

'What a to-do, Miss Templeton!' she exclaimed, her hands flapping in front of her bosom. 'Nora is all of a tremble and here's you all shook up as well. Taylor will have something to say to young Higgins if it turns out to be lack of care on his behalf! Now, let's get you upstairs to your room so we can ascertain the damage.'

Lucy was torn between protesting herself fit enough to walk up the stairs unaided or making use of the convenience of her reaction to the shock of being thrown on to the floor of the carriage. Her body didn't seem to be quite its normal self and she chose the latter, but felt compelled to intervene on Higgins' behalf.

'No, no! No blame can be attached to Higgins for the carriage accident. His driving was exemplary. In fact, his careful handling of the horses prevented a much worse outcome, I am sure.' She didn't want to voice her suspicions of sabotage in the presence of the servants, but she was sure that a close examination of the vehicle would prove her suspicions.

'Never mind that for now, Miss Templeton. Mr Cunningham will see to everything that's necessary. Follow me, Jones and Brown.'

At that, Mrs Hardy swept up the stairs, with the two footmen valiantly trying to keep up with her. Once in Lucy's room, they lowered her feet to the ground, allowed her to gain her balance and immediately bowed their exit.

Lucy was surprised to find her legs were trembling and that she was barely able to sustain her balance. Mrs Hardy steadied her and led her to the bedside chair.

'Let's get you disrobed, Miss Templeton and then you will be able to rest to recover from the shock of the accident,' she soothed her. 'One of the maids will be up directly and we can get you tucked up into bed in no time at all. Did you bang your head at all?'

'Only a little,' Lucy confessed, not wanting a great fuss made of her. 'I am just a little shaky, that's all. I am sure a hot drink of something will make me as right as rain again. Maybe I could then be left to rest in quietness?' She needed to be alone, to decide what to do. What bad luck that Rupert had joined Marissa at the home of the Darlingtons. He was the only one she felt at liberty to confide in.

'You are looking rather flushed,' Mrs Hardy commented as she slipped Lucy's carriage gown over her head. 'No doubt you are also over-excited by your parents' imminent arrival. Does your head ache?'

Lucy's concern – and her mental efforts to devise a suit-able plan of action – was indeed making her head ache and she admitted as much.

'Then I suggest you remain in your bed for the remainder of the day, Miss Templeton.' She smiled kindly, as she held out Lucy's nightrobe. 'I will tell Cook to make you some beef tea and then you will probably find a short sleep will do you the world of good. You will ring for assistance if you need anything?'

'Yes, indeed. Thank you, Mrs Hardy.'

Lucy lowered herself to the bed and allowed Mrs Hardy to help her to raise her legs and tuck the blankets around her. She leaned back against the pillows, thankful for the moment that someone else was making the decisions for her. After fussing about for a few more minutes, Mrs Hardy was satisfied that she could do no more for Miss Templeton's comfort and she quietly left the room.

Lucy was on her own at last. She needed to plan exactly how she was going to accomplish what she knew she must do but she felt surprisingly languid. She forced her mind to stay alert.

One option, of course, was to send word to the local magistrate, but, on such slender evidence, he would think her a buffle-headed miss who had nothing better to do than to dream up a complete bag of moonshine.

No, in Rupert and Marissa's absence, she must creep out of the house and go up to the Hall to see if Lord Rockhaven were already there, or if Tomkins was expecting his master to return that night. If, by chance, Lady Montcliffe was there, Lucy felt sure her past acquaintance would mitigate any offence her uninvited visit might cause. But first, she must just close her eyes for a little while to clear this muddleheaded mist that seemed to want to envelop her....

Lucy awoke and lay still for a moment. A slight sound made her aware that someone was in her room and she opened her eyes. Why was she in bed? It didn't seem to be the right time of day, although she could tell it was dark outside.

It was Nora. 'Are you awake, miss? I hope I didn't disturb you, only Cook told me to bring up your tray, Miss Templeton, as Peggy is cleaning the silver. It's a bowl of beef tea. Shall I put it here, miss?'

At Lucy's assent, the maid carefully put the tray on the

bedside table. 'I hope you're soon feeling better, miss. Is there anything else I can do for you while I'm here?'

Lucy shook her head. 'No, thank you, Nora. But surely you should be resting, too. You had just as great a shake up as I did.'

Nora gave a small laugh. 'Eeh, no, miss. With all the preparations for Lord and Lady Templeton's arrival tomorrow, there ain't enough of us to give me time off, besides, Cook said as 'ow sitting with you would be giving me a rest, like. She said as I was to make sure you 'ad this beef tea and then settle you down to sleep. And she said as I could sit in the chair by your side to make sure you're all right.'

Oh, dear! That was unfortunate. Whilst Nora had been talking, Lucy had remembered her plans for the evening, but she hadn't considered the likelihood of having the presence of a maid to overcome. 'What hour is it, Nora?' she asked, not sure how long she had been asleep.

'It must be about six, miss. Cook was just saying 'ow fortunate it is that she didn't 'ave to break off the preparations for tomorrow to make the children's nursery tea and then cook Mr and Mrs Cunningham's dinner with them all being out at the party. We'd normally be in the thick of it all by now!'

'Hmm! Why don't you just give me the bowl of beef tea and then go and lie down in your own bed?' Lucy suggested. 'I am sure that would be much more comfortable for you.'

'Eeh, I couldn't do that, miss! Cook'ud likely get me dismissed!' Nora protested. 'No, I must stay 'ere. I'll be as quiet as I can, miss. I won't disturb you.'

Lucy felt in a quandary. She didn't want to involve Nora

in her misdeed but could really see no option. Besides, it would be comforting to share her concerns. 'The thing is, Nora,' she began, 'there's somewhere I really must go this evening.' And she quickly explained what she had to do.

Nora was horrified. 'Eeh, no, miss! You can't do that!'

'I must, Nora. Lord Rockhaven's life is in danger.'

Nora was literally wringing her hands. 'No, you must wait until Mr Cunningham comes home, miss!'

'I can't. We don't know how long he will be.'

'Then tell Farrell, miss. He'll know what to do.'

'No, I daren't risk it. He will react just as you have. And there's no one else. I've got to go myself. I'll be all right, really I will. Now, you must help me get dressed, Nora. The sooner I go, the sooner I will be back.'

'Ohh, miss! Don't do it. There'll be trouble.'

Lucy swung her legs out of bed. 'Either you help me, or I dress on my own. Either way, I have made up my mind – I must go and warn Theo … that is, his lordship. You can help me … and you'll be able to stop anyone coming in to see if I am all right.' Lucy was now warming to this slight change of plan. 'You'll be able to tell them I am sleeping and say that they mustn't disturb me. Now, come on, Nora, get my old carriage dress out of the wardrobe for me.'

'Oh, miss!' Nora did as she was told, protesting her reluctance all the while. 'I'll lose me job, miss, you just wait and see.'

'No, you won't. If we are discovered I shall say that I *made* you obey me … which is true.' She took off her nightgown and held out her arms for Nora to slip her shabby carriage dress over her. Her head felt as though it didn't quite belong to her, but that was probably the excitement of what she was about to do. 'But I hope we won't be discovered. I shall warn whoever I find up at the Hall and will come home directly. If we roll up some clothing and put it in my bed, if anyone comes, they will think it is me and will leave me to sleep until morning.'

'At least put on your cloak as well, miss, it'll be right cold out there.'

'That's a good idea … and the hood will shield my face in case any other traveller catches sight of me.' Not that she expected to see anyone, but it would be best if she could blend into the background of trees once out of the house. A young lady out on her own at this time of day would attract attention and she didn't want anyone to question her, or offer to convey her wherever she was going.

'Oh, don't say that, miss!' Nora wailed.

'You're right. We won't even think it!' Lucy soundly affirmed. 'Now, all I have to do is to get out of the house without being seen. Don't forget to roll up some clothing, Nora and then make yourself comfortable in the chair.' She hesitated and then put her arms around Nora and hugged her. 'I *have* to do this, Nora,' she assured the maid earnestly. 'And I promise, that if anything should go wrong, I will make sure that you are not blamed. I promise you. All right?'

Nora gulped and nodded. 'All right, miss. I'll do as you say.'

Lucy let go of her and tiptoed to the bedroom door. All was quiet outside her room. She crept to the top of the stairs. Not a sound to be heard. It was an ideal time with her sister's family still out visiting and the servants busy in the kitchen.

Luck was on her side. She crept quietly down the stairs and out through a side door. She had already dismissed the idea of going to the stables to ask for Maud to be harnessed to the gig. Even though the head groom was still out with the family coach, no one would suppose it acceptable for her to be going out at this time of day, almost midway through December, and it would involve yet more of the servants in her escapade. No, she would have to walk.

Through the wood was the shortest way, but a mist was curling through the shrubbery and she didn't feel bold enough to enter the wood on her own. It would be easy to miss her way if the mist thickened. Going by the road was the better choice. She didn't imagine there would be many vehicles and, if one should happen along, she would hear it coming and could quickly slip into the trees that bordered the lane.

Her heart was beating rapidly, but she told herself that the journey was really no different than it would be in daylight. All she had to do was keep a tight hold on her imagination and everything would be all right.

Theo had laid his plan well. He had enough contacts from his days with the military to be able to choose reliable men to make enquiries quietly and feed back the information via Boulton and Dodds. He knew his cousin had received the information that he was returning on his own to Montcliffe Hall today and he had no doubt but that he would take the bait and make a move against him. And he was pretty certain that that move would be during the journey. Piers would not wait until he was back in residence with faithful retainers around him.

He also knew which stretch of road Piers would most likely choose for his ambush. It was after a series of twists in the road, which any driver of repute would negotiate with care, just before the road straightened out and the coach would pick up speed. The area was wooded with both trees and shrubs, giving cover to anyone of a mind to take advantage. That's where *he* would choose, were he in his cousin's shoes. Though Piers hadn't been the wiliest of soldiers, surely even he would be capable of making that decision.

It also gave cover to anyone who wished to observe such an act and catch the perpetrator red-handed! Just in case, Theo had placed a few men stationed at other positions. The route had been well covered, but Theo now eyed his companion with grim satisfaction. They had silently watched Piers take up his position nearer to the road with a number of companions, all of whom were under surveillance by Theo's men and would be silently put out of action when the affray began, especially the thug who was Piers's former batman. Two men had been assigned to disable *him*. Now was the hardest part: waiting.

Both Theo and his companion were dressed in dark brown and, leaning against the sturdy tree as they were, blended in with their surroundings. It took self-control to keep still and not to give in to the urge to swing their arms about themselves or to stamp their feet to restore the circulation and Theo hoped his companion was not suffering unduly. He was the local magistrate; an older man, but necessary to Theo's plan. He was counting on the surprise of being thwarted in his plan would cause Piers to be indiscreet with his words.

He hated this part of any engagement. Nerves were on edge, wondering how it would go. It was always thus when campaigning. Once the battle started, training kicked in and the instinct to out-manoeuvre the enemy took over. To kill or be killed was easier then, with no time to be afraid.

It was cold. He blew into his hands silently, temporarily warming them.

A sharp sound in the distance brought all his senses together. His muscles tensed. A coach was approaching. Was it *his* coach? His ears listened intently, telling him four horses were in harness. He could imagine every twist in the road as the sounds came closer. This was it!

A few hundred yards or so away, Lucy increased her pace, even though the ground was now rising slightly. The coach had passed her a moment before. She had heard it coming long before it swayed round the intervening bend and she had had plenty of time to drop into the roadside ditch and crouch in its shadows. She raised her head as it passed and she recognized the Montcliffe coat of arms emblazoned on its doors.

Her head was full of questions. Should she have taken a chance and stopped it *en route*? She dismissed that thought; there was no way of knowing which coach it was until it drew level and it would have been too late to draw back if it were another. By the time she had scrambled back up on to the road, the rear of the coach was already lost in swirls of mist, the rumble of the wheels fading as it went around the bend at the top of the slope.

Was Theo a passenger inside it? He could be driving into danger. Was he well? Fully recovered? She hoped so. Surely he wouldn't have planned his return unless he was. Did he know that his cousin was back in the area? What if he didn't? She must hurry!

Her footwear was totally unsuited to running and it wasn't an activity she had indulged in very much in recent years. Well-brought-up young ladies weren't expected to run. Nor were they given the opportunity. Even her outings in the wood with the children hadn't prepared her muscles for the exertion now required of them, and the carriage accident earlier in the day had affected her strength more than she had realized at the outset, but her anxiety spurred her on her way. Hurry! Hurry! 'Please be safe, Theo!'

A pistol shot rang out through the misted air. The sound momentarily froze her steps. A stab of fear pierced her heart. She heard the panicky sound of horses missing step and rearing and the jangle of harness out of rhythm.

With a small cry, she urged her feet onwards, her breath now coming in painful gasps. As she stumbled round the next curve in the road, she was brought to an abrupt halt.

Twilight was settling upon the day but there was enough light remaining for her to make out the silhouetted shape of the large coach. It had been forced to stop. A bulky man, whom she presumed was the driver, lay sprawled face down on the ground, dangerously near the horses' hoofs. A rough-looking individual was trying to hold the bridles of the frightened leading horses, whilst another, with a heavy cudgel in his hand, stood over the fallen man. Was either of them the rough-looking groom whom she had seen with Potterill on that first occasion? He would be a brutal opponent.

As she crept forward, she could see another man by the

side of the coach. From his height and build, she knew it was Lieutenant Potterill. Her breath seemed to be stuck in her throat and her mind paralyzed. What was he going to do? If Theo were indeed in the coach, why hadn't he leaped out to see what was going on? Was there a possibility that he wasn't in it? Or had he already been injured by that pistol shot she had heard?

Before her thoughts had had time to settle, Potterill yanked open the door, but stepped back a pace when the cloaked figure of a woman appeared in the doorway of the coach. She heard Potterill stammer, 'A … Aunt Isabelle!' followed by, 'Really, Piers! Whatever is happening?' It was the countess, without any trace of fear in her voice. 'What are you doing here? I think I heard a shot. Have we been held up?'

At the same moment another dark form emerged from the shelter of the trees to her left and a commanding voice rang out, 'Hold it right there, Piers! You are surrounded!'

Lucy recognized the voice and turned in consternation as she realized the second dark figure was Theo, miraculously standing unaided. His right arm was outstretched, a pistol pointing straight at his cousin. She realized that Theo had challenged his cousin before he had had time to see his mother framed in the doorway of the coach. He clearly had no idea that she would be there, or he would have challenged his cousin before he had opened the door.

Yet another dark form emerged behind Theo a few yards to his left as, with a swift movement, Piers reached forward and grabbed hold of the countess, dragging down her slender form from the coach. He held her against his body, a pistol to her head.

'Don't move, anyone, or I shall shoot her!'

Lucy held her breath, her eyes locked on Potterill. The muzzle of his pistol was pressing against Lady Montcliffe's temple as his glance darted between Theo and his companion. 'Throw down your pistols where I can see them!' he shouted.

Lucy gasped. If Theo did as he was bidden, he would be at his cousin's mercy. In a flash of understanding, Lucy knew Piers would then kill all present to silence them and, no doubt, lay the blame on a marauding band of thieves! She knew no one dared to move just as she also knew Theo *would* throw down his pistol as he had been ordered, in the hope of saving his mother.

Fourteen

L ucy knew she was the only one who could do anything! But what?

Out of the corner of her eye she saw the man who had dealt with the coach driver begin to creep around the back of the coach. She didn't dare wait until he entered the fray. She needed to distract Piers in order to give Theo a chance to save his mother without sacrificing himself.

She stooped down and groped her fingers over the ground until she felt a large stone. She swiftly scooped it up and, imagining that she were bowling over-arm to someone taller than Bertie, she flung it over everyone's heads to land in the only direction where no one was standing. It hit against the trunk of a tree with a sharp crack!

Instantly, Potterill swung around to face that direction, sweeping the light figure of the countess off her feet with him, and fired his pistol. Immediately, another shot rang out. Potterill staggered sideways and fell against the body of the coach, dragging Lady Montcliffe with him. As they collapsed to the ground, Theo lurched forward, followed by his companion.

There were sounds of other scuffles and fights going on in the shrubbery across the road, but Lucy's attention was solely upon the fallen figures on the ground by the coach.

She ran forward, also. 'Is Lady Montcliffe all right?' she gasped.

Theo didn't respond. Instead, he stamped his foot on his cousin's outstretched hand that still loosely held his pistol. The precaution wasn't necessary. Potterill remained slumped where he had fallen.

'A good shot,' Theo's companion murmured quietly. 'He deserved it, the scoundrel.'

The countess, with Lucy's help, was struggling to sit up. 'Thank you, my dear.' Her eyes widened in surprise. 'Lucy! You are the last person I expected to see!'

Until Lady Montcliffe spoke her name, Theo's attention had been solely upon his mother. He had bent awkwardly over her, the pain in his back preventing him from being able to lift her to her feet. He turned in amazement, involuntarily wincing as he straightened.

'Lucy? Miss Templeton?' He looked back at his mother, who was now leaning on Miss Templeton's arm as she regained her feet. He put out a hand to steady her, holding on to the coach door with his other hand. 'You know Miss Templeton, Mama?'

'Yes, dear. She was a guest at the Hall just over a year or so ago.'

'Oh, look out!' Lucy clutched at his arm as the man with the cudgel came into view. They weren't yet out of danger!

Theo tensed for action but immediately relaxed. 'It's all right, he's one of my men.'

'Oh! But I thought—!'

'So did Piers,' Theo said with a note of satisfaction in his voice. He looked at the man. 'How's Simkins? Not too stunned, I hope?'

'Nah, he'll do, 'Twas naught but a tap,' the man replied, his swarthy face softened by a grin. 'I managed to warn him and he dropped like a professional!'

Lucy's eyes were drawn to the still figure on the ground. 'He's dead, isn't he? Will you get into trouble for killing your cousin? Although, everyone will give witness—'

'The shot was mine,' the other man interrupted. He bowed briefly towards Lady Montcliffe. 'William Grantham, ma'am. The local magistrate. I'll take full responsibility for what has happened. Full warning was given and he chose to ignore it. Now, if everyone agrees, it's time we moved on. The night's drawing in and it's getting damnably cold! Get these ladies sorted out, Rockhaven, and leave the rest of us to do what we have to here.'

His words reminded Lucy of the impropriety of her presence. 'Oh, yes, I must return home immediately!' she cried with dismay. Now that the danger was over, her legs seemed to want to crumple beneath her, but she was too proud to admit to such weakness. Her other predicament, that of being missed from her room, was of much more importance. 'No one knows I am out of the house,' she added ruefully. She turned to Lady Montcliffe, stricken by embarrassment. 'Please don't think badly of me for being out at this hour with no maid in attendance! I simply couldn't think of any other way to warn Theo ... that is, Lord Rockhaven ... that his cousin was back in the area.'

'Ha! If you think yourself wanton for being out without a maid in attendance,' Theo declared, 'look no further than at my dear mother! The coach was *supposed* to be *empty*, Mama!'

'*Touché!*' Lady Montcliffe laughed, not in the least embarrassed. 'Yes, I'm sorry I nearly wrecked your plan. I thought my presence might defuse the situation, but I see I was wrong. Do you think he would really have killed me? Yes, I see you do.' For a moment she seemed overtaken by shock, but she pulled herself together and resorted to admonition. 'You should have told me in greater detail what you were planning! I just couldn't wait tamely in London knowing that you were planning to somehow lure Piers into making a move against you, and I could hardly put any of my maids into such a dangerous position, could I? However, it is only for one night. They are following on tomorrow. In the meantime, Miss Templeton, Theo and I will escort you back to Glenbury Lodge, so that we can explain what has happened to your sister.'

Lucy would have liked nothing better than to arrive home sheltered by the countess's presence, and that of her son, but she would prefer it if Marissa and other members of her sister's household did not discover her evening's deception quite so dramatically. Besides, she must protect Nora's part in her deception.

'Please, no!' she implored. 'I am in disgrace enough, as it is. My sister is out visiting and I am supposed to be resting in my room after a ...' No, she mustn't mention the carriage accident. That would complicate the matter and delay them all departing to their homes. 'I pretended to be a little unwell so that I could come to warn Lord Rockhaven that his cousin was in the area trying to recruit men to assist him. Everyone thinks I am asleep in my bed. I am hoping to be back in my room before Marissa returns. She will be shocked if she hears of my part in this, and my maid is covering for me. It will be much better if I creep back into the house unnoticed. I can be back home by the time you have turned the coach around. Oh dear, it all sounds quite dreadful of me. I'm sorry. I just didn't know what to do.'

Theo reached out to touch her arm, his face wincing in pain with the sudden movement. 'It was very brave and resourceful of you, Miss Templeton, but you must allow me to come with you to make sure of your safety.'

Lucy backed away, shaking her head, knowing that if he touched her, she would lose her resolve. His pain was evident and Lady Montcliffe seemed as if she had borne enough for one night. 'No! Your mother's need is greater than mine. I'm just so glad you're safe, m'lord!'

Their gaze met and held for a few seconds, each conveying a tumult of emotion. Lucy longed to be held in his arms, to feel his strong body against hers, except, right now, he *wasn't* strong. The strained lines of his face showed that his exertions had taken their toll on him and she knew he wouldn't want her to witness his physical weakness.

'It isn't far ... and it's mostly downhill,' she said, forcing a light laugh. 'I'll be home before you are.'

'Then one of my men will escort you as far as the door. I insist.'

Lucy agreed. She was sorry to have to leave. She wanted to hear all the details. Where had Theo been during the past few weeks? How did he know his cousin was going to waylay him on his return to Montcliffe Hall? But, most of all, she just wanted to feast her eyes on him and take in the fact that he was back on his feet and able to walk unaided.

'Are you sure this is what you want to do, my dear?' Lady Montcliffe asked. 'I will defend your action to your sister. Without your distraction, I am sure Piers would have killed my dear Theo. His men' – she gestured around at the small band of men now standing around awaiting their orders what to do next – 'were as helpless to do anything to save me as he was as they were at the other side. I am eternally grateful to you, my dear.'

But Lucy was adamant. The consternation that would be brought on by Lady Montcliffe arriving unannounced on the doorstep of Glenbury Lodge in such circumstances was more than she could bear to contemplate. 'Yes,' she said firmly, covering her head with the hood of her cloak. 'This is best.'

Theo took hold of her hand and bowed over it. 'I will call tomorrow, as soon as I am able,' he said softly, raising her hand to his lips. His glance seemed to hold a hint of promise and Lucy felt her heart quicken. It was enough.

She bobbed a tiny curtsy and then, with an air of more confidence than she truly felt, she turned away and, with one of Theo's men loping along at her side, she hurried down the hill to Glenbury Lodge. Slivers of light shone through the gaps in the curtains at the downstairs windows. She hoped it meant only that the servants had everything ready for their mistress's return. All she needed to do was to get upstairs without being seen.

Her heart thumped uncomfortably as she approached the side door through which she had left the house just over an hour earlier. Would it still be unlocked? She tested the handle and breathed a sigh of relief. It was just as she had left it. Silently signalling to the man who had accompanied her that his duty was now over, she gently pushed open the door and slipped inside. She closed the door quietly behind her and momentarily leaned back against it. Her heart was racing but she mustn't linger. In complete darkness, she softly made her way along the short corridor to another door that led into a carpeted hallway. Once there, she felt sure she would be able to detect if anyone were in the vicinity though, hopefully, all would be quiet.

It was not to be. It was a swing door and, as she tentatively pushed it forward, it was whisked from her hand and she stumbled forward into the well-lit hallway. Her brother-in-law, Rupert, faced her angrily.

'So, you are back! There had better be a good explanation for this, my girl!'

'Yes, Rupert, I'm—'

But, without giving Lucy a chance to start explaining, he grasped her arm and marched her into the main part of the house. Ignoring the shocked faces of the few servants they passed, he hurried her down the main hallway and flung open the drawing-room door, thrusting her into the room before him.

'Here she is!' he snapped. 'And look at the state of her!'

Marissa had obviously been pacing up and down the room in a state of agitation. Now, she halted and whirled around to stare at her sister, aghast at what she saw. Her hand flew from clutching the necklace at the base of her throat to cover her mouth, her eyes wide with consternation. But, as Lucy lifted her chin to face her, a mixture of dismay, regret and defiance in her expression, she realized that Marissa wasn't the only person in the room. Rising from their seats by the fire were Lord and Lady Templeton, their faces equally shocked and angry.

'Mama! Papa!' She felt what remained of her spirit plummet. Oh, dear! This was going to be far worse than she could have ever imagined.

Marissa strode forward and pulled Lucy further into the room. 'Lucy, how could you? Where have you been? Just *look* at her, Mama! She'll be the ruin of us! And the servants! I hope the servants haven't seen her!' Marissa's voice rose into a wail.

Lucy tried to tug her arm free of her sister's grasp, but her mama's, 'Oh, Lucy!' brought her resistance to a standstill. The reproach in her voice tore at her heart.

'I'm sorry, Mama. I didn't mean you to see me like this. I hoped to be back before anyone missed me. You weren't meant to arrive until tomorrow.' It wasn't what she had meant to say but the shock of seeing her parents here had robbed her brain of reason.

'Then it's as well we came a day early, isn't it?'

Her mama's face hardened and she glared at Lucy's state of dishevelment. 'Just look at you! I can't believe that a daughter of mine can bear to be seen in such disarray. Your dress is filthy and torn! Your hair is all over the place and your face is flushed! I don't know if I even *want* to hear what you have been up to.'

'I had to go,' Lucy cried. 'I had to warn him ... to try to save him ... and I did! It was his cousin, you see.' Her words were coming out all wrong but Lucy couldn't help it. 'He'd already tried—'

Marissa latched on to one word. 'Him? Him? You have been with a man? Who is he? Nurse Harvey has said all along that you have been a bad influence on the children, and now Arabella tells me you have befriended a pirate in the wood and have been visiting him! And taking the children with you! Tell me, if you can, that it wasn't he whom you have been with tonight.'

'Well, yes, but it's not—'

'Ohh! I knew it! You wicked girl! Did you hear that, Rupert? She has led my innocent children astray and I will never forgive her, Mama. I've tried to do my best for her, but I've failed!' Marissa flung herself weeping into her husband's arms.

'No, listen, Marissa. You don't understand. He's not a pirate, he's—'

'Silence, Lucy!' her father thundered. 'I will not have any more of your wilful excuses. I determined to listen to you, to hear what you had to say for yourself, as I have always done in the past, but this is the final indignity you will heap upon us. No, don't interrupt! I will have my say! Neither your mama nor I will put up with it any longer! Now, go to your room and do not emerge from it until you are bidden. We will discuss what is to be done with you tomorrow.'

'But—!' Lucy tried to speak again.

'Go!' he thundered again, his arm dramatically pointing towards the door.

Lucy knew better than to continue to defend herself. It would only make her papa more angry. Near to tears, her whole body trembling, she summoned enough strength to hold her head high. Her face drained of all colour, she reached out her hand in an impassioned plea towards her mother but she just stared at her coldly. With a broken sob, Lucy turned away and fled to her bedroom. Nora was no longer there. Lucy could only presume that her maid's part in her deception had been discovered and that she also would be facing punishment.

*

The following day, a silent maid brought a breakfast tray into Lucy's bedroom. Lucy didn't know her and the maid made it clear that she was not to speak to her nor answer any questions.

Lucy drank the milk but the bread stuck in her throat and she was barely able to swallow it. She rehearsed in her mind all that she needed to say to her parents, to explain how she met Lord Rockhaven in the gamekeeper's cottage and how she had inadvertently become involved in the attempt made on his life there, and how she had once again, quite accidentally, seen his cousin Piers at The Red Fox and overheard him trying to hire men to aid him in killing Lord Rockhaven. Surely they would then understand why she had acted as she did, especially after Piers Potterill had sabotaged her carriage and could have caused the death of any of its three occupants.

It was late morning when she was summoned to present herself in the drawing room. Both her parents were there and Marissa and Rupert. Only her papa was standing. Her mama and Marissa were seated on a sofa, their faces strained with anxiety; Rupert was sitting on an upright chair, trying to appear nonchalant and relaxed, but appeared to Lucy to be poised ready to spring forward at any given moment. The tension in his face revealed how severely he regarded the misdemeanours that had taken place under the shelter of his guardianship, under his roof, undermining his respectability – she could almost hear the words in his mind. Yet she didn't altogether blame him. Without knowing the circumstances, what had happened must seem a bit bizarre and unwarranted.

'You may sit down, Lucy,' her papa invited, indicating

another upright chair, appropriately placed in front of the others. Lucy seated herself on its edge, feeling as if she were a prisoner on trial, facing the jury.

'So, I trust you have had time to reflect upon your actions, Lucy. What have you to say for yourself? Give us some reason that might enable us to comprehend how a young woman of your class and upbringing can feel free to flout all that has been instilled into you about what is acceptable behaviour and what is not, for, try as I might, I cannot, at this moment, think of any mitigating circumstances.'

Lucy haltingly began, recounting that first day when Wellington had bounded off, following the scent of rabbit stew, with Bertie hot on his heels, how she and Arabella had followed, hoping to catch up with them before they left the confines of the wood.

'Don't you dare blame my children, Lucy!' Marissa cried. 'They were *innocents* in your care.'

'I'm not *blaming* them. I'm trying to *explain*,' Lucy defended herself. 'It wasn't planned, it just happened! Only Bertie was at the gamekeeper's cottage before we caught up with them and then Lord Rockhaven came round the corner in a chair of wheels and the chair toppled over, tipping him out on to the cobbles. He couldn't get up and—'

'Lord Rockhaven?' her mama squealed. 'You have been consorting with Lord Rockhaven in the woods … on his land? Theodore Montcliffe? He of renown as a rake and wild libertine? A reputed coward, drummed out of his regiment for desertion of duty? Oh, it gets worse and worse! My salts! Where are my salts, Marissa?'

'I wasn't *consorting* with him, Mama! I felt it was our fault … my fault,' Lucy amended at a further cry from

Marissa, 'that his chair overturned and so I felt compelled to try to help him get up. Only I couldn't, so I wrapped his coat around him and waited until his servant returned.'

'And Lord Rockhaven let you? He was so careless of your reputation that he lay there and allowed you to minister to him, unchaperoned?' Lord Templeton queried with incredulity in his voice.

'Well, he didn't exactly *want* me to,' Lucy remembered. 'But, what else could I do? It was our fault it had happened. I couldn't just leave him, could I?'

'You shouldn't even have been there,' Rupert reminded her coldly.

'Well, no, but we were, so I had to make the best of it.'

'Or the worst,' Marissa accused. 'You have always managed to find yourself in the midst of a scrape.'

'This is worse than a *scrape*!' Rupert reminded her. 'This is social suicide. And it will rebound on us and our children's future. Mud sticks, as you well know.'

Lord Templeton made an impatient gesture at Rupert's dire warnings and turned back to Lucy. 'So Lord Rockhaven is the pirate that Bertie confessed to knowing. Didn't you think it odd that an earl should be living in disguise and skulking in his gamekeeper's cottage on his own land, instead of residing in comfort up at the Hall? Didn't that tell you that this was a man not to be trusted? A man who might even have to find a way of silencing you and the children?'

Lucy almost laughed. 'He wasn't skulking in disguise. His patch covers his damaged eye. He was badly injured on the Peninsular. He has a scar on his face and he couldn't walk. He was trying to recover his strength before his cousin found him – the same cousin who had already killed Conrad and shot Theo in the back!'

'*Theo*, is it?' Rupert again interrupted patting his wife's hand as she let out a wail of horror as Lucy described the earl's injuries. 'How far have things gone between you? I never got closer than calling him Rockhaven.'

Lord Templeton waved a hand at him impatiently. He preferred to concentrate on the other details in his daughter's attempt to rationalize her actions. 'Lord Rockhaven was shot in the back as he deserted the battle-field,' he contradicted her, 'He used his brother as a shield and Conrad was fatally wounded. Even his mother couldn't face the shame of it all and has been living in obscurity in their London house.'

'No!' Lucy cried. 'He didn't! His cousin had already shot Conrad and Theo was trying to save him! And Lady Montcliffe wasn't ashamed of him, she came—'

'Psh! This is getting us nowhere,' Lord Templeton inter-rupted. 'From what you are saying, you must have made other trysts in the wood with him … and last night? What was that all about? Daytime assignations are bad enough, but it is beyond the pale to go out alone to meet him in the near dark.'

'I didn't go to meet him. I told you, I went to try to *warn* him. I knew his cousin was back in the area, trying to recruit men to help him in his attempt to get rid of Theo. I asked Higgins to listen to what he was saying.'

'And that's another thing, involving my servants in your meddling schemes!' Marissa complained. 'Well, they've been dismissed as an example to the others!'

'What?' cried Lucy. 'You can't! They were trying to help me!'

'Higgins single-handedly wrecked our barouche, almost killing all three of you, and Nora tried to conceal your duplicity! They would have helped you better by refusing to go along with your meddling schemes!'

'But that's not fair! I think Lieutenant Potterill somehow sabotaged the barouche. He caused the accident, not Higgins. Higgins did nothing wrong.'

'Quiet, Lucy!' her papa bade her. 'You must accept, that, by involving them, you implicated them and encouraged them to be disloyal to their true employers. Out of misplaced loyalty to you, they didn't report your behaviour. Rupert had to make an example of them. Their dismissal is a burden you will have to bear and maybe the memory of it will encourage you to modify your behaviour in future.'

'I can't believe you are doing this, Papa! Higgins only did as I asked; he didn't know that I intended to go up to Montcliffe Hall.'

'But Nora did! And she aided and abetted you! I can't believe, Lucy, that you think so little of your reputation ... and that of your family ... that you have deliberately flaunted yourself with this known degenerate reprobate and believed his cock-and-bull story about his cousin trying to kill him. It is far more likely that this cousin was trying to restore some honour to the family name.'

'You are wrong, Papa,' Lucy's voice was quiet as she faced her papa, determined to make him understand. 'Lieutenant Potterill *did* try to kill Lord Rockhaven and Lady Montcliffe, but it was he who ended up being killed. He was shot.'

Lady Templeton's face blanched and a sound like the moan of an animal in distress sounded in her throat. 'You saw a man killed? Last night? Lord Rockhaven killed his cousin? And you were a party to it? Oh, Lucy, what have you done?' She reached out a hand beseechingly towards her younger daughter, but her strength failed her and she sank back against the sofa. 'Oh, Edmund! What are we to do?'

'Do?' repeated Lord Templeton. 'We will do the only thing left for us to do! We will return to our home immediately and send word to Herbert Murchison that we accept his offer of marriage to our daughter. If we can get the announcement in the *Gazette* before news of all this scandal breaks, it will go some way to calm the waves.'

'No, Papa!' Lucy cried. 'You can't do that! I won't marry Herbert Murchison! He's old! You can't make me! Besides, I … I love Lord Rockhaven … and I believe he loves me. He said he will come to see you as soon as he is able. He *will* come, I know he will!'

'That man will not be allowed over my threshold,' Rupert declared. 'He is a disgrace to the peerage.'

Lucy shook her head. 'Have you not listened to a word I have been saying? Lord Rockhaven is an honourable man. He does not deserve your censure.'

Lady Templeton smiled sadly. 'It is now late morning and, although it is early for social calls, if he were as eager to stand by your side as you say he is – and ready to face our wrath – he would be here by now. But, he is not. I think it is safe to say that gentlemen do not marry young ladies who romp with them in the wood – not even if their own reputation hangs by a thread, as does the Earl of Montcliffe's.'

Even Marissa looked appalled by her father's decision. 'Oh, Papa, Herbert Murchison is over forty. He has bandy legs and has lost most of his hair. You can't make Lucy marry *him*!'

'I can and I will. He is a sincere young man of thirty-eight years and is the second son of a baronet. He is of very sound character *and* he is the only man who has made an offer since Lucy was compelled to cut short her Season.'

Lord Templeton glared at each one in turn, as if daring any to voice further opposition. 'In the light of all this, I am not risking a second Season ending up as disastrously as her first. My mind is made up. I am sorry to spoil your Christmas, Marissa, but we must leave immediately and get the betrothal announced before news of this scandal breaks. The servants will have packed our things by now. All that is needed is for us to change into our travelling clothes.'

Lucy was shocked. 'I won't go! And I won't marry him! I would rather enter a convent!' she declared passionately.

Lord Templeton eyed her coolly. 'If I were you, young lady, I would be careful what alternatives you offer, for it may turn out to be the only course left to you!'

Fifteen

IT WAS LATE morning when Theo awakened. His back had been in an agony of pain for hours and it was well into the early hours of the morning before he fell into an exhausted sleep.

His restless hours had not been total agony, however. He smiled as he recalled the various times he had had the pleasure of the delightful and somewhat unconventional Miss Templeton's company. Not that every meeting had been an episode of sweetness and delight, however. He frowned when he thought of how morose he had been at their first meeting. Would she hold that against him? Did she find him a boorish man? He hoped not. He hadn't been at his best at that first meeting, but he felt he had improved since. What a strange hand of fate it was that his tumble from his wheelchair had released a trapped nerve and allowed movement to return to his legs.

But what had he to offer such a lovely young girl – apart from his wealth and title – but, somehow, he didn't think *that* would sway Miss Templeton if her heart said otherwise. She didn't appear to mind his injuries, not even his disfigured face, which wasn't a pretty sight first thing in the morning. He groaned. How could he contemplate

inflicting such scarred features on to such a delightful crea-
ture? Was he out of his mind? Probably, he admitted
ruefully, because he was certainly going to give it a try –
even if he had to endure the torment of a Season on the
marriage mart whilst he courted her and attempted to win
her heart.

He laughed aloud as he recalled his dear mama telling
him late last night of his grandmother's roguish attempt to
matchmake between the two of them. What had his mama
said? Grandmother had asked Miss Templeton if she would
marry her eldest grandson and Miss Templeton had
replied, 'Not unless I loved him.' *Did* she? Did he *dare* hope?

He was going to find out and as soon as possible. He
swung his legs out of bed and stretched his limbs before
carefully rising to his feet and commencing the series of
movements he had devised to loosen and strengthen his
body. His mobility was getting better every day and, in spite
of the tension in his muscles from the previous day's activities, he knew he was well on the way to full recovery, even
if he did still need the help of a cane. Life was suddenly
looking good, but it wouldn't be perfect until he knew where
he stood with the delightful Miss Templeton and only then
if she felt the same way about him as he did about her.

Good heavens! He felt as nervous as a young buck about
to make his first declaration. No, that wasn't true, he felt
more nervous, because he knew that this was no passing
fancy. He loved her. She was everything he wanted and
needed. He felt he had known her longer than the actual
reality of a few months. She had been hovering as a
tangible wisp of a dream that floated on the edge of his
consciousness for a couple of years, just waiting for fate to

take a hand in bringing them together. Her image had danced and floated in his arms in his pain-filled nightmares; someone who had drawn him back from the depths of oblivion after the debilitating injuries inflicted by his cousin Piers; someone who had soothed away the devastating pain when he had been told of Con's death – only he hadn't known her face, just the sense of her presence ... a presence that always faded in his first moments of waking, like the remnant of a dream.

But now she was real. He knew her name; he knew her face; and he would see her again – today!

Suddenly eager to set his plans into motion, he strode into his dressing room calling for Crawford, his valet. He could tell by the sounds of activity within the Hall that it must be nearly time for nuncheon already. He would go the moment he had eaten.

In the event, it was two o'clock in the afternoon when his coach swept through the gates of Glenbury Lodge. Amazingly, a groom or gardener was there ready to open the gates and Simkin was able to maintain the pace of his matching four without them breaking step. It was almost as if he were expected, though the Cunninghams' butler took a moment to recognize him.

'Lord Rockhaven! My, but it's good to see you, m'lord! We heard your return was imminent!' the butler exclaimed a few seconds after he stepped through the doorway. His face resumed its trained neutrality as he added sombrely, 'My condolences about your brother, m'lord.'

Theo nodded, silently accepting the condolences. It didn't get any easier.

There was something odd about the butler's demeanour

though, Theo thought, as he watched the butler recollect his duties and make his way along the reception hall and knock discreetly on a door halfway down its length. The initial glow of pleasure that broke through the butler's practised passive expression, a glow that had given him hope of a good reception from the Cunningham's themselves, had been swiftly replaced by a hint of wariness, apprehension, even, something more than the swift recognition of his need to rely upon the supporting aid of his cane. No doubt whispers of the previous night's happenings had begun to filter through the amazing network of communication that the servants in neighbouring houses seemed to have with each other.

He wasn't kept waiting long. He heard a murmur of voices, a low feminine cry of – was it consternation? Then the deeper, soothing tones of a masculine murmur. He wondered what Lucy … Miss Templeton … had told them; how much had she shared? Were they expecting him? Or were they hoping Lord and Lady Templeton would be here before he made his call? Miss Templeton had said they were expected later today, had she not?

Maybe he had been too precipitous. No, he felt the circumstances demanded an urgent visit, if only to declare his good intentions. Other, more formal visits would be needed in due time, of course, but he was eager to see the delightful Miss Templeton again, utterly confident that he had never met any other who could hold a candle to her. Life with her would never be mundane, of that he was sure!

Ah, the butler was returning.

'Mr and Mrs Cunningham will receive you, m'lord. Will you come this way?'

Leaning heavily on his stick, Theo followed him back to the drawing room, hoping that he would find Miss Templeton there also.

'Lord Rockhaven, Earl of Montcliffe,' the butler announced and Theo advanced into the room. He was glad that he had made good use of his enforced absence from Society to replenish his wardrobe. Although he had regained much of the weight lost at the height of his convalescence, his clothes had hung upon him as if adorning a scarecrow, causing Crawford, to shudder with distaste. But, today he was dressed as fine as any gentleman should be, in a well-cut coat of plum-coloured superfine, a neatly tied cravat, biscuit-coloured pantaloons and gleaming Hessian boots. He held his hat and gloves as he made a fine bow.

There was a strained air between the couple, though they made every effort to hide it as they echoed their butler's greetings and condolences. However, Cunningham's bow was no more than perfunctory, though he couldn't fault Mrs Cunningham's curtsy. Indeed, she seemed reluctant to rise from it and, when she did, she seemed reluctant to meet his glance. He was aware that his eye-patch was causing Mrs Cunningham some problems, too. She kept glancing at it and then sliding her glance away again, as she twisted and untwisted a lace-edged kerchief in her hands. Theo bore it ruefully, knowing it was something he would have to cope with until people became accustomed to seeing his disfigurement.

His hostess perched herself on the edge of a straight-backed seat, stiffly indicating that he do likewise. 'Please be seated, m'lord. You will partake of some refreshment?'

Theo flicked back the tails of his coat and carefully sat

down. 'If you please, ma'am.' He glanced about him, imagining Miss Templeton gracing the room with her lively presence. 'What a pleasant room you have here.'

After enduring ten minutes of excruciating conversation, Theo knew the allotted time for making a call was passing by. He must ask to see Miss Templeton before society manners compelled him to make his departure.

'And your sister, Miss Templeton, is staying with you, I believe,' he enquired casually.

'Lucy?' Mrs Cunningham almost squeaked, casting an alarmed glance at her husband, whom Theo had to admit had been devilishly sullen throughout the conversation.

Theo bowed his head in assent. 'I have had the pleasure of making Miss Templeton's acquaintance and would like to pay my respects ... if she is at home to visitors this afternoon.'

'No! You cannot!' Mrs Cunningham said abruptly, her fingers spread at the base of her throat. 'You have been misinformed, m'lord! She isn't here!'

'Not here?' Theo looked from his hostess to her husband. 'But she *has* been here! When did she leave?'

Mrs Cunningham threw a despairing glance at her husband, who took it upon himself to make a brief reply.

'She left, with her parents, about half an hour ago, m'lord, just before you arrived.'

Theo swore mildly under his breath. Her parents had arrived and removed their daughter immediately? The outdoor man had been *closing* the gates, not opening them! He forced his voice to remain calm as he asked, 'And when will she return?'

'Miss Templeton will not be returning in the foreseeable

future, my lord,' the honourable Rupert said tersely.

'What?' Theo couldn't believe it. He had been wasting valuable time! He hurriedly rose to his feet, but before he could say another word, a scuffle in the doorway heralded the arrival of both a maid with a tray of refreshments and an excited boy, whom Theo recognized immediately.

'Rocky!' Bertie exclaimed. 'I knew it must be you when Farrell teased me that you look like a pirate. Aunt Lucy said you had gone, but I knew you'd come back! I hoped so, anyway.'

'Bertie! You should not be in here! Where is Nurse Harvey?' Rupert Cunningham reprimanded him sternly.

Bertie's face fell. 'I'm sorry, Papa. I wanted to see Rocky.' He turned to face him again. 'Did you know that Aunt Lucy has gone away, now, sir? She'll be so sorry to have missed you. She was crying, you know. It made me sad to see her crying … and now Bella's crying upstairs in the nursery. But I didn't cry … well, not very much.' His face brightened again. 'I know! Do you want to come and see Wellington? I'm teaching him to pretend to be dead when I tell him to! You'll see how much he has improved since you last saw him.'

Before Theo could reply, an older woman entered the room looking flustered. 'I'm terribly sorry, ma'am, sir, your lordship. He just ran off, ma'am. Come back to the nursery at once, Master Bertie, if you please!'

'Thank you, Nurse Harvey,' Mrs Cunningham said faintly, fanning her hot cheeks with her hand.

'Go at once, Bertie!' his father commanded.

'I will see Wellington next time I call, Bertie,' Theo promised, as the downcast boy was hustled from the room by his nurse.

'You promise?'

'I promise.'

'See! I told you he was kind,' Bertie's voice floated back through the doorway before Farrell drew it closed.

Theo eyed his disconcerted hosts. 'I know I owe you an explanation, but there isn't time, right now. Forgive my hasty departure. I must leave at once.'

'I forbid you to follow my sister-in-law, my lord!' Rupert said stiffly. 'I don't know what sort of *acquaintance* you have with her, but it seems to me—'

'She saved my life last night!' Theo said sharply. 'And our *acquaintance* has been totally honourable!' He swung around to face Mrs Cunningham. 'In which direction have they gone, ma'am?'

'Er ...' She cast an anxious glance at her husband. 'To our country estate in Surrey, my lord.' She glanced at her husband again before adding hastily, 'My parents plan to marry her to a middle-aged neighbour without delay.'

'Ha! Do they, indeed?'

He couldn't resist grinning mischievously at her over his shoulder as he hurried to the door. 'Somehow, I think that highly unlikely!'

He nodded a hasty farewell to Farrell and hurried down the steps as fast as he was able with his slightly ungainly gait, glad to see that Simkin had already turned the coach. 'The Surrey road, Simkin,' he ordered as he clambered inside. 'As fast as you can!'

He was possibly about forty-five minutes behind Miss Templeton and her parents. He couldn't begin to imagine what had taken place in the Cunninghams' home last night, or earlier today, but he gathered that his dear love had been taken home in some sort of disgrace because of her association with him. Marry her off to a middle-aged neighbour, indeed! Not while he had a breath of life in his body!

It was about an hour and a half later when Simkin bellowed that their quarry was in sight. Theo's heart was racing. Had he read Miss Templeton's sentiments towards him correctly? He hoped so; a Season in London wasn't one of his priorities.

His coach swiftly overtook the rear of the Templetons' two coaches and gradually drew level with the larger town coach Theo was pursuing. Theo looked through the near-side window, hoping to catch a glimpse of Miss Templeton. His heart leaped with joy. She was seated at the off-side, facing the rear, gazing with unseeing eyes through the window. The sight of her pale face, her eyes large and brimming with tears, tore at his heart. The coaches kept pace with each other and Theo saw the moment when her gaze, initially with casual uninterest, focused upon his face. He smiled and raised his hat, watching her expression change, running through surprise, disbelief, dawning belief, incredulity, into, wonderfully, rapturous delight! He saw her body straighten as her lips formed the shape of his name. 'Theo!'

Simkin needed no instructions. He raised his hat to the Templeton coachman, shouted, 'Pull to!' and drew slightly ahead, drawing closer to the Templetons' coach, setting a line that would force the other coach off the road if it kept to its present course, leaving the other coachman no alternative than to haul back on the reins.

As soon as Simkin drew the horses to a halt, Theo moved as quickly as he was able, but not as swiftly as Lucy.

She was out of her seat before the coach had drawn to a halt, her hand on the handle, ready to open the door.

'Sit down at once, Lucy!' Lady Templeton commanded her daughter.

Her father banged on the coach roof. 'What's happening, Bradley?'

'It's Lord Rockhaven,' Lucy informed them, as she opened the door. She glanced back over her shoulder as she made to leap down without waiting for the step to be lowered. 'I knew he'd come for me. And he has!'

'Don't be ridiculous, Lucy! Don't you dare…! Come back, Lucy!' her mother cried.

Lucy paid no heed. She nimbly jumped from the coach and ran forward to where Theo was carefully stepping down from his coach. 'You came!' she cried with delight. 'I hoped you would. And dreaded you wouldn't.'

She paused, suddenly shy. He looked … different. A tiny gasp caught in her throat. He was no longer dressed in the garb of a rough soldier hiding in the woodland. Instead, he looked rather splendid in his well-tailored coat and tightly fitting pantaloons. His cravat was of plain cream silk but fell in well-ordered folds. Was he still the man she had fallen in love with?

She suddenly wondered if her greetings were a little too presumptuous, but before her doubts had time to take root, he was standing before her and immediately drew her into his arms. 'How could I not, my darling girl?'

She looked adorable. Her hesitancy made her seem vulnerable and he longed to sweep her up into his arms and twirl her around. He longed to capture her laughing red lips in his own and taste the sweet delight of her, but he wasn't yet strong enough for such flamboyant behaviour and he was conscious that her father was descending from his coach with an expression of wrath upon his face. So, instead, he held her at arm's length and then took hold of one hand.

'Lucy, I mean, Miss Templeton, I will court you through the next Season if I must, but I can't wait to know. Can you bring yourself to love me? Can I hope?'

Lucy beamed up at him, her eyes shining, though she tried to look stern. 'Ugh! Not another Season. I hoped for better than that from you, m'lord!'

'Ah! Not a long courtship, then?' With a wary eye on the approaching Lord Templeton, he raised his right eyebrow and cupped her chin in his hand, lowering his head until his breath whispered across her lips. 'How short?'

Lucy felt ready to melt. Her limbs were turning to jelly and her heart was racing wildly out of control. She felt euphoric. She was in his arms again, at last. She remembered his last kiss. She held her breath, revelling in the warmth of his breath on her lips.

'*Very* short?' she whispered.

'Christmas, then. We'll be married at Christmas.'

'Oh, yes!'

'You, sir!' Lord Templeton thundered. 'Unhand my daughter!'

Theo stepped to the side, but kept hold of Lucy's right hand. He made a brief but pleasant obeisance with his other hand.

'Lord Templeton … Lord Rockhaven, Earl of Montcliffe, at your service, sir! May I speak to you, concerning your daughter's hand in marriage?'

Lord Templeton looked ready to splutter an outraged refusal, but Lucy slipped her hand free of Theo's and ran to her father. She slipped her arm into his and looked up at him beguilingly.

'Do say yes, Papa, for you must know that I love him dearly!'

'Hmph! Love, indeed!' Lord Templeton eyed Lord Rockhaven speculatively. An earl, eh? And Murchison was merely the second son of a baronet. And, if Lucy's wild revelations were to be believed, Montcliffe wasn't the disgraced soldier he had been rumoured to be. Besides, he knew a *fait accompli* when he saw one. He nodded curtly. 'Instruct your driver to follow us to our home, m'lord. I will speak to you there.'

Later, in front of a roaring fire in the Templetons' drawing room, Theo took hold of Lucy's hand and drew her to him. He had already assured her that he appreciated loyal servants and that her erstwhile maid and groom would be welcomed into his household. His heart swelled with love for her. He would give her *everything* that was in his power to give.

Lucy felt a melting deep within her as she willingly stepped into the circle of his arms, loving the way her body moulded to his shape, loving the very essence of him: the scent of his skin, the re-growing strength of his muscles, the very masculinity of him. She knew she was where she always wanted to be.

She lifted up her face and smiled shyly.

He was watching her changing expressions, his eyes reflecting her look of love and longing. His lips curled upwards and crinkly lines radiated outwards from the corners of his eyes, both the one she could see and the one behind the patch. He lowered his head towards her, until his lips moved softly over hers, caressing them, teasing them; the tip of his tongue flickered, begging entrance until, with a tiny sigh, her lips parted and his tongue probed gently, meeting hers with a thrill of joy, causing the kiss to deepen; a long slow kiss that set Lucy tingling from the top of her head to the soles of her feet.

A tiny moan of contentment and desire for more sounded in her throat, causing Theo to draw her body closer to him. Strange sensations swept though Lucy's body, hot and melting, low in her abdomen, where she could feel the hardness of his body pressing against her own yielding softness.

She longed to know where this yearning was taking her – wherever it was, she knew she would have to wait, but not for too long, she hoped. She knew it was going to be the most wonderful thing she would ever experience and her heart flooded with love for him.

When they needed to breathe, Theo raised his head. 'Why do I feel we have done this before?'

Lucy laughed, her eyes dancing with delight. So he did remember ... somewhere deep inside. Her fingers entwined in the hair at the nape of his neck. She had longed to do that so many times, that and other exciting things.

She drew his head back towards her.

'I'll tell you later,' she breathed softly. 'But, right now ... ohhh!'

NEATH PORT TALBOT LIBRARY
AND INFORMATION SERVICES

1		25		49		73
2		26		50		74
3		27		51		75
4		28		52	2111 76	
5		29		53		77
6		30		54		78
7	9/10	31		55		79
8		32		56		80
9		33		57		81
10	.	34		58		82
11		35		59		83
12		36		60		84
13		37		61		85
14		38		62		86
15		39		63		87
16		40		64		88
17		41		65		89
18		42		66		90
19		43		67		91
20		44		68		92
21		45		69		COMMUNITY SERVICES
22		46		70		
23		47		71		NPT/111
24		48		72		.